SYLVIA TOWNSEND WARNER

(1893-1978) was born in Harrow, the daughter of George Townsend Warner, housemaster and Head of the Modern side of Harrow. As a student of music she became interested in research in the music of the fifteenth and sixteenth centuries, and spent ten years of her life as one of the four editors of the ten-volume compilation *Tudor Church Music*. In 1925 she published her first book of verse, *The Espalier*. With the publication of the novels *Lolly Willowes* in 1926, *Mr Fortune's Maggot* and *The True Heart* in the two following years, she achieved immediate recognition. The short stories she contributed to the *New Yorker* for over forty years established her reputation on both sides of the Atlantic.

In 1927 Sylvia Townsend Warner visited New York as guest critic for the *Herald Tribune*. In the 1930s she was a member of the Executive Committee of the Association of Writers for intellectual liberty and was a representative for the Congress of Madrid in 1937, thus witnessing the Spanish Civil War at first hand.

In all, Sylvia Townsend Warner published seven novels, four volumes of poetry, a volume of essays, and eight volumes of short stories. Her biography of T. H. White, published in 1967, was acclaimed in the *Guardian* as one of the two most outstanding biographies to have appeared since the war.

A novelist of formidable imaginative power, each of Sylvia Townsend Warner's novels is a new departure, ranging from the revolutionary Paris of 1848 in *Summer Will Show* (1936), a 14th-century Abbey in *The Corner That Held Them* (1943) to the South Seas Island of *Mr Fortune's Maggot*, and 19th-century rural Essex in *The True Heart*. The two latter novels, published by Virago, are outstanding examples of Sylvia Townsend Warner's startling originality, wit and style.

Sylvia Townsend Warner lived most of her adult life with her close companion Valentine Ackland, in Dorset, then in Norfolk and later in Dorset once again where she died on 1 May 1978, at the age of eighty-five.

If you would like to know more about Virago books, write to us at 41 William IV Street, London WC2N 4DB for a full catalogue.

Please send a stamped addressed envelope

MR. FORTUNE'S MAGGOT

✦

SYLVIA TOWNSEND WARNER

✦

To Theo

Published by VIRAGO PRESS Limited 1978
41 William IV Street, London WC2N 4DB

Reprinted 1983

First published 1927 by Chatto & Windus Limited
Copyright ©|Sylvia Townsend Warner 1927

British Library Cataloguing in Publication Data
Warner, Sylvia Townsend
  Mr Fortune's maggot. —(Virago modern classics)
  I. Title
  823′.912[F]   PR6045.A12
  ISBN 0-86068-043-6

Printed in Great Britain by litho at
The Anchor Press, Tiptree, Essex

*The scenes and characters of this story are entirely
imaginary. In the island names the vowels should be
pronounced separately with the Italianate vowel-sounds.
Words of three syllables are accented on the second:
Fanùa, Luèli.*

*I am greatly obliged to Mr. Victor Butler for his
assistance in the geometrical passages, and for the
definition of an umbrella.*

PREFACE

In 1918 when I first went to live in London, at 127 Queens Road, I was poor and thought I could not afford a Times Book Club subscription. I soon exhausted my own books, and though I had the British Museum by day I wanted something to read in the evening. Then I happened on the Westbourne Grove branch of the Paddington Public Library. It was a very down-at-heel establishment, with a great many bad biographies of unimportant people, and all the books had the same smell (I suppose it was some public disinfectant). I found it very convenient, and used it hard. One of the books I borrowed was a volume of letters by a woman missionary in Polynesia. I can't remember the title, or her name; but the book pleased me a great deal, it had the minimum of religion, only elementary scenery, and a mass of details of every-day life. The woman wrote out of her own heart – for instance, describing an earthquake, she said that the ground trembled like the lid of a boiling kettle.

In 1925 I had finished *Lolly Willowes*, and was writing poetry and a few short stories when one early morning I woke up remembering an extremely vivid dream. A man stood alone on an ocean beach, wringing his hands in an intensity of despair; as I saw him in my dream, I also knew something of his circumstances. He was a missionary, he was middle-aged, and a deprived character, his name was Hegarty, he was on an island where he had made only one convert: and at the moment I saw him he had just realised that the convert was no convert at all. I jumped out of bed and began to write it down, and even as I wrote a great deal which I had known in the dream began to scatter; but the main facts, and the man's loneliness, simplicity, and despair, and the look of the island, all remained as actual as something I had really experienced.

With the minimum of fuss I made a few notes of the development, discarded the name of Hegarty because it might lead me into a comic Irishman, and began to write. The opening, up to Lueli's baptism, is, with scarcely a word's alteration, as I wrote it down. This must have been in winter, because I remember Duncan Grant coming to dinner on the same day, and we had the gas fire on, and ate some sort of stewed game. The moment he had gone I went on writing.

My remembrance of the book from the Paddington Public Library was so vivid and substantial that I never felt a need to consult any other books. The lady's account of the earthquake I could supplement by Bea Howe's remembrance of the Valparaiso earthquake: this gave me the lamp beginning to swing. The public library lady also gave me the lava in the water flowing towards the south. The idol I had from the missionary's cottage at Wayford in Somerset which I hired for the summer of 1926. The parrot lived next door to this cottage, and I grew very familiar with its voice in a tree, and noticed how much quieter unconfined parrots sound.

There had been some breaks between when Duncan came to dine and when I was at Wayford; but after that I wrote steadily, and with increasing anxiety; not because I had any doubt about the story, but because I was so intensely conscious that the shape and balance of the narrative must be exactly right – or the whole thing would fall to smithereens, and I could never pick it up again. I remember saying to Bea that I felt as if I were in advanced pregnancy with a venice glass child. It was made the more alarming by the way in which things kept on going right – like the business of Mr Fortune's watch, for instance. I was really in a very advanced stage of hallucination when I finished the book – writing in manuscript and taking wads of it to be typed at the Westbourne Secretarial College in Queens Road.

I remember writing the last paragraph – and reading over the conclusion, and then impulsively writing the envoy, and beginning to weep bitterly.

I took the two copies, one for England and one for USA to Chatto and Windus myself. I was afraid to trust them by post. It was a very foggy day, and I was nearly run over. I left them with a sense that my world was now nicely and neatly over.

Sylvia Townsend Warner, Dorset, 1978

MR. FORTUNE'S
MAGGOT

MAGGOT. 2. A whimsical
or perverse fancy; a crotchet.
N.E.D.

Though the Reverend Timothy Fortune
had spent three years in the island
of Fanua he had made but one convert.
Some missionaries might have been galled
by this state of things, or if too good to be
galled, at least flustered; but Mr. Fortune was a humble man of heart and he had
the blessing which rests upon humility: an
easy-going nature. In appearance he was
tall, raw-boned, and rather rummaged-
looking; even as a young man he had learnt
that to jump in first doesn't make the 'bus
start any sooner; and his favourite psalm
was the one which begins: 'My soul truly
waiteth still upon God.'

Mr. Fortune was not a scholar, he did
not know that the psalms express bygone
thoughts and a bygone way of life. In his

literal way he believed that the sixty-second psalm applied to him. For many years he had been a clerk in the Hornsey branch of Lloyds Bank, but he had not liked it. Whenever he weighed out the golden sovereigns in the brass scales, which tacked and sidled like a yacht in a light breeze, he remembered uneasily that the children of men are deceitful upon the weights, that they are altogether lighter than vanity itself.

In the bank, too, he had seen riches increase. But he had not set his heart upon them : and when his godmother, whose pass-book he kept, died and left him one thousand pounds, he went to a training-college, was ordained deacon, and quitted England for St. Fabien, a port on an island of the Raratongan Archipelago in the Pacific.

St. Fabien was a centre of Christianity. It had four missions : one Catholic, one Protestant, one Wesleyan, and one American. Mr. Fortune belonged to the Protestant mission. He gave great satisfaction to his superiors by doing as he was bid, teaching in the school, visiting the sick, and carrying the subscription list to the English visitors, and even greater satisfaction when they had discovered that he could keep all the accounts. At the end of ten years Archdeacon Mason was sorry to hear that Mr. Fortune (who was now a priest) had felt a call to go to the island of Fanua.

Fanua was a small remote island which could only be seen in imagination from that beach edged with tin huts where Mr. Fortune walked slowly up and down on evenings when he had time to. No steamers called there, the Archdeacon had visited it many years ago in a canoe. Now his assistant felt a call thither, not merely to visit it in the new mission launch, but to settle there, and perhaps for life.

The two clergymen strolled along the beach in the cool of the evening. The air smelt of the sea, of flowers, and of the islanders' suppers.

' I must warn you, Fortune, you are not likely to make many converts in Fanua.'

' What, are they cannibals ? '

' No, no ! But they are like children, always singing and dancing, and of course immoral. But all the natives are like that, I believe I have told you that the Raratongan language has no words for chastity or for gratitude ? '

' Yes, I believe you did.'

'Well, well! You are not a young man, Fortune, you will not expect too much of the Fanuans. Singing and dancing! No actual harm in that, of course, and no doubt the climate is partly responsible. But light, my dear Fortune, light! And not only in their heels either.'

'I am afraid that none of the children of men weigh altogether true,' said Mr. Fortune. 'For that matter, I have heard that many cannibals are fond of dancing.'

'Humanly speaking I fear that you would be wasted in Fanua. Still, if you have felt a call I must not dissuade you, I won't put any obstacles in your way. But you will be a great loss.'

The Archdeacon spoke so sadly that Mr. Fortune, knowing how much he disliked accounts, wondered for a moment if God would prefer him to wait still in St. Fabien. God tries the souls of men in crafty ways, and perhaps the call had been a temptation, a temptation sent to try his humility. He turned his eyes towards where he knew the island of Fanua to lie. What his superior had said about it had not displeased him, on the contrary he liked to think of the islanders dancing and singing.

It would be a beautiful estate to live among them and gather their souls as a child gathers daisies in a field.

But now the horizon was hidden in the evening haze, and Fanua seemed more remote than ever. A little cloud was coming up the heavens, slowly, towards the sunset ; as it passed above the place of Fanua it brightened, it shone like a pearl, it caught the rays of the sun and glowed with a rosy rim. Mr. Fortune took the cloud to be a sign.

Heartened by a novel certainty that he was doing the right thing, he disappointed the Archdeacon quite unflinchingly and set about his preparations for the new life. Since the island was so unfrequented it was necessary to take with him provisions for at least a year. In the ordinary course of things the Mission would have supplied his outfit, but he had a scruple against availing himself of this custom because, having kept the accounts, he knew their poverty and their good works, and also because he was aware that the expedition to Fanua was looked on as, at best, a sort of pious escapade. Fortunately there were the remains of his godmother's legacy. With feelings that were a

5

nice mixture of thrift and extravagance he bought tinned meat, soup-squares, a chest of tea, soap, a tool-box, a medicine chest, a gentleman's housewife, a second-hand harmonium (rather cumbrous and wheezy but certainly a bargain), and an oil-lamp. He also bought a quantity of those coloured glass baubles which hang so ravishingly on Christmas trees, some picture-books, rolls of white cotton, and a sewing-machine to make clothes for his converts. The Archdeacon gave him a service of altar furniture and the other mission-workers presented him with a silver teapot. With the addition of some plate-powder Mr. Fortune was now ready to embark.

In fancy he had seen himself setting foot upon the island alone, though he knew that in fact some one must go with him if only to manage the launch. But that some one would be a sailor, a being so aloofly maritime as scarcely to partake in the act of landing. He was slightly dashed when he discovered that the Archdeacon, accompanied by his secretary, was coming too in order to instal him with a proper appearance of ceremony.

' We cannot impress upon them too early,'

said the Archdeacon, ' the solemn nature of your undertaking.' And Mr. Fortune hung his head, a grey one, old and wise enough to heed an admonition or a rebuke.

The voyage was uneventful. The Archdeacon sat in the bows dictating to the secretary, and Mr. Fortune looked at the Pacific Ocean until he fell asleep, for he was tired out with packing.

About sunset he was aroused by the noise of surf and by peals of excited laughter ; and opening his eyes he found that they were close in under the shadow of the island of Fanua. The launch was manœuvring round seeking for an inlet in the reef, and the islanders were gathered together to view this strange apparition. Some were standing on the rocks, some were in the sea, others were diving from cliff to water, in movement and uproar like a flock of seagulls disturbed by a fishing-boat.

It seemed to Mr. Fortune that there must be thousands of them, and for a moment his heart sank. But there was no time for second thoughts ; for behold ! a canoe shot forward to the side of the launch, a rope was thrown and caught, the Archdeacon, the secretary, and himself were miraculously jumped in, the sea was alive with brown heads, every one talked at once, the canoe turned, darted up the smooth back of a wave, descended into a cloud of spray, and the three clergymen, splashed and stiff, were standing on the beach.

Now Mr. Fortune was properly grateful for the presence of the Archdeacon, for like a child arriving late at a party he felt perfectly bewildered and would have remained in the same spot, smiling and staring. But like the child at a party he found himself taken charge of and shepherded in the right direction until, in the house of the chief islander, he was seated on a low stool with his hat taken off, a garland round his neck, and food in his hands, smiling and staring still.

Before dark the luggage was also landed. The evening was spent in conversation and feasting. Every one who could squeeze himself into Ori's house did so, and the rest of them (the thousands did not seem above a few hundreds now) squatted round outside. Even the babies seemed prepared to sit there all night, but at length the Archdeacon, pleading fatigue, asked leave of his host to go to bed.

Ori dismissed the visitors, his household prepared the strangers' sleeping place, unrolling the best mats and shooing away a couple of flying foxes, the missionaries prayed together and the last good-nights were said.

From where he lay Mr. Fortune could look out of the door. He saw a tendril of some creeper waving gently to and fro across the star Canopus, and once more he realised, as though he were looking at it for the first time, how strangely and powerfully he had been led from his native land to lie down in peace under the constellations of the southern sky.

' So this is my first night in Fanua,' he thought, as he settled himself on his mat. ' My first night . . .'

And he would have looked at the star, a sun whose planets must depend wholly upon God for their salvation, for no missionary could reach them ; but his eyes were heavy with seafaring, and in another minute he had fallen asleep.

As though while his body lay sleeping his ghost had gone wandering and ascertaining through the island Mr. Fortune woke on the morrow feeling perfectly at home in

Fanua. So much so that when he stood on
the beach waving farewell to the launch he
had the sensations of a host, who from seeing
off his guests turns back with a renewed
sense of ownership to the house which the
fact of their departure makes more deeply
and dearly his. Few hosts indeed could
claim an ownership equally secure. For
when the Archdeacon, visited with a sudden
qualm at the thought of Mr. Fortune's
isolation, had suggested that he should come
again in three months' time, just to see how
he was getting on, Mr. Fortune was able
to say quite serenely and legitimately that
he would prefer to be left alone for at least
a year.

Having waved to the proper degree of
perspective he turned briskly inland. The
time was come to explore Fanua.

The island of Fanua is of volcanic origin,
though at the time of Mr. Fortune's arrival
the volcano had been for many years
extinct. It rises steeply out of the ocean,
and seen from thence it appears dispropor-
tionately tall for its base, for the main peak
reaches to a height of near three thousand
feet, and the extremely indented coast-line
does not measure more than seventy miles.

On three sides of the island there are steep cliffs worked into caverns and flying buttresses by the action of the waves, but to the east a fertile valley slopes gently down to a low-lying promontory of salt-meadow and beach where once a torrent of lava burst from the side of the mountain and crushed its path to the sea ; and in this valley lies the village.

The lower slopes of the mountain are wooded, and broken into many deep gorges where the noise of the cataract echoes from cliff to cliff, where the air is cool with shade and moist with spray, and where bright green ferns grow on the black face of the rock. Above this swirl and foam of tree-tops the mountain rises up in crags or steep tracts of scrub and clinker to the old crater, whose ramparts are broken into curious cactus-shaped pinnacles of rock, in colour the reddish-lavender of rhododendron blossoms.

A socket of molten stone, rent and deserted by its ancient fires and garlanded round with a vegetation as wild as fire and more inexhaustible, the whole island breathes the peculiar romance of a being with a stormy past. The ripened fruit falls from the tree, the tree falls too and the ferns leap up from it as though it were being consumed with green flames. The air is sleepy with salt and honey, and the sharp wild cries of the birds seem to float like fragments of coloured paper upon the monotonous background of breaking waves and falling cataract.

Mr. Fortune spent the whole day exploring, and when he felt hungry he made a meal of guavas and rose-apples. There seemed to be no end to the marvels and delights of his island, and he was as thrilled as though he had been let loose into the world for the first time. But he returned with all the day's wonders almost forgotten in the excitement and satisfaction of having discovered the place where he wanted to live.

It was a forsaken hut, about a mile from the village and less than that distance from the sea. It stood in a little dell amongst the woods, before it there was a natural lawn of fine grass, behind it was a rocky spur of the mountain. There was a spring for water and a clump of coco-palms for shade.

The hut consisted of one large room opening on to a deep verandah. The framework was of wood, the floor of beaten earth, and it was thatched and walled with reeds.

Ori told him that it could be his for the taking. An old woman had lived there with her daughter, but she had died and the daughter, who didn't like being out of the world, had removed to the village. Mr. Fortune immediately set about putting it in order, and while he worked almost every one in the island dropped in at some time or other to admire, encourage, or lend a hand. There was not much to do : a little strengthening of the thatch, the floor to be weeded and trodden smooth, the creepers to be cut back—and on the third day he moved in.

This took place with ceremony. The islanders accompanied him on his many journeys to and from the village, they carried the crate containing the harmonium with flattering eulogies of its weight and size, and when everything was transported they sat on the lawn and watched him unpacking. When he unpacked the teapot they burst into delighted laughter.

Except for the lamp, the sewing-machine, and the harmonium, Mr. Fortune's house had not an European appearance, for while on the island he wished to live as its natives did. His bowls and platters and drinking·

vessels were made of polished wood, his bed (Ori's gift) was a small wooden platform spread with many white mats. When everything was completed he gave each of the islanders a ginger-bread nut and made a little formal speech, first thanking them for their gifts and their assistance, and going on to explain his reasons for coming to Fanua. He had heard, he said, with pleasure how happy a people they were, and he had come to dwell with them and teach them how they might be as happy in another life as they were in this.

The islanders received his speech in silence broken only by crunching. Their expressions were those of people struck into awe by some surprising novelty : Mr. Fortune wondered if he were that novelty, or Huntley and Palmers.

He was anxious to do things befittingly, for the Archdeacon's admonition on the need for being solemn still hung about the back of his mind. This occasion, it seemed to him, was something between a ceremony and a social function. It was a gathering, and as such it had its proper routine : first there comes an address, after the address a hymn is sung, then comes a collect and sometimes a collection, and after that the congregation disperses.

Mr. Fortune sat down to his harmonium and sang and played through a hymn.

His back was to the islanders, he could not see how they were taking it. But when, having finished the hymn and added two chords for the Amen, he turned round to announce the collect, he discovered that they had already dispersed, the last of them even then vanishing noiselessly and enigmatically through the bushes.

The sun was setting behind the mountain, great shafts of glory moved among the topmost crags. Mr. Fortune thought of God's winnowing-fan, he imagined Him holding the rays of the sun in His hand. God winnows the souls of men with the beauty of this world : the chaff is blown away, the true grain lies still and adoring.

In the dell it was already night. He sat for a long time in his verandah listening to the boom of the waves. He did not think much, he was tired with a long day's work and his back ached. At last he went indoors, lighted his lamp and began to write in his diary. Just as he was dropping off to sleep a pleasant thought came to him,

and he smiled, murmuring in a drowsy
voice : ' To-morrow is Sunday.'

In the morning he was up and shaved
and dressed before sunrise. With a happy
face he stepped on to his lawn and stood
listening to the birds. They did not sing
anywhere near so sweetly as English black-
birds and thrushes, but Mr. Fortune was
pleased with their notes, a music which
seemed proper to this gay landscape which
might have been coloured out of a child's
paint-box.

He stood there till the sun had risen and
shone into the dell, then he went back
into his hut ; when he came out again he
was dressed in his priest's clothes and carried
a black tin box.

He walked across the dell to where there
was a stone with a flat top. Opening the
box he took out, first a linen cloth which he
spread on the stone, then a wooden cross
and two brass vases. He knelt down and
very carefully placed the cross so that it
stood firm on the middle of the stone. The
vases he carried to the spring, where he
filled them with water, and gathering some
red blossoms which grew on a bush near by
he arranged them in the vases, which he

then carried back and set on either side of the cross. Standing beside the stone and looking into the sun, he said in a loud voice : 'Let your light so shine before men, that they may see your good works, and glorify your Father which is in heaven.'

The sun shone upon the white cloth and the scarlet flowers, upon the cross of wood and upon the priest standing serious, grey-headed and alone in the green dell all sparkling with dew as though it had never known the darkness of night.

Once more he turned and went back to the hut. When he came out again he carried in either hand a cup and a dish which shone like gold. These he put down upon the stone, and bowed himself before them and began to pray.

Mr. Fortune knelt very upright. His eyes were shut, he did not see the beauty of the landscape glittering in the sunrise, the coco-palms waving their green feather head-dresses gently to and fro in the light breeze, the wreaths of rosy mist floating high up across the purple crags of the mountain— and yet from the expression on his face one would have said that he was all the more aware of the beauty around him for having his eyes shut, for he seemed like one in an ecstasy and his clasped hands trembled as though they had hold of a joy too great for him. He knelt on, absorbed in prayer. He did not see that a naked brown boy had come to the edge of the dell and was gazing at him and at the stone which he had decked to the glory of God—gazing with wonder and admiration, and step by step coming softly across the grass. Only when he had finished his prayer and stretched out his hands towards the altar did Mr. Fortune discover that a boy was kneeling at his side.

He gave no sign of surprise, he did not even appear to have noticed the newcomer. With steadfast demeanour he took from the dish a piece of bread and ate it, and drank from the cup. Then, rising and turning to the boy who still knelt before him, he laid his hand upon his head and looked down on him with a long look of greeting. Slowly and unhesitatingly, like one who hears and accepts and obeys the voice of the spirit, he took up the cup once more and with the forefinger of his right hand he wrote the sign of the cross upon the boy's forehead with the last drops of the wine.

The boy did not flinch, he trembled a

little, that was all. Mr. Fortune bent down and welcomed him with a kiss.

He had waited, but after all not for long. The years in the bank, the years at St. Fabien, they did not seem long now, the time of waiting was gone by, drowsy and half-forgotten like a night watch. A cloud in the heavens had been given him as a sign to come to Fanua, but here was a sign much nearer and more wonderful : his first convert, miraculously led to come and kneel beside him a little after the rising of the sun. His, and not his. For while he had thought to bring souls to God, God had been beforehand with His gift, had come before him into the meadow, and gathering the first daisy had given it to him.

For a long while he stood lost in thankfulness. At last he bade the kneeling boy get up.

' What is your name ? ' he said.

' Lueli,' answered the boy.

' I have given you a new name, Lueli. I have called you Theodore, which means " the gift of God." '

Lueli smiled politely.

' Theodore,' repeated Mr. Fortune impressively.

The boy smiled again, a little dubiously this time. Then, struck with a happy thought, he told Mr. Fortune the name of the scarlet blossoms that stood on either side of the cross. His voice was soft and pleasant, and he held his head on one side in his desire to please.

' Come, Theodore, will you help me to put these things away ? '

Together they rinsed the cup and the dish in the spring, folded the linen cloth and put them with the cross and the vases back into the black tin box. The flowers Mr. Fortune gave to the boy, who with a rapid grace pulled others and wove two garlands, one of which he put round Mr. Fortune's neck and one round his own. Then discovering that the tin box served as a dusky sort of mirror he bent over it, and would have stayed coquetting like a girl with a new coral necklace had not Mr. Fortune called him into the hut.

In all Lueli's movements there was a swiftness and a pliancy as though not only his mind but his body also were intent on complaisance and docility. A monkey will show the same adaptability, deft and pleased with his deftness, but in a monkey's face there is always a sad self-seeking look, and his eyes are like pebbles unhappily come alive. Birds, or squirrels, or lizards whisking over the rock have a vivid infallible grace ; but that is inherent, and proper to their kind ; however much one may admire or envy them, they do not touch one into feeling grateful to them for being what they are. As Mr. Fortune watched Lueli folding up the priestly clothes, patting them smooth and laying them in their box, he felt as though he were watching some entirely new kind of being, too spontaneous to be human, too artless to be monkey, too sensitive to be bird or squirrel or lizard ; and he wished that he had been more observant of creation, so that he could find out what it was that Lueli resembled. Only some women, happy in themselves and in their love, will show to a lover or husband this kind of special grace ; but this Mr. Fortune, whose love affairs had been hasty and conventional, did not know.

While they were breakfasting together in the verandah the missionary had a good look at his convert.

Lueli was of the true Polynesian type, slender-boned and long-limbed, with small

idle hands and feet : broad-minded persons
with no colour prejudices might have described him as aristocratic-looking. This
definition did not occur to Mr. Fortune,
who had had no dealings with aristocrats
and was consequently unaware of any
marked difference between them and other
people ; but he reflected with satisfaction
that the boy looked very refined for one
who had been so recently a heathen. His
eyes were rather small and his nose was
rather snub, but these details did not mar
the general good effect of regular features
and a neatly shaped head. Though when
he talked he pulled very charming faces, in
repose his expression was slightly satirical.
In colour he was an agreeable brown,
almost exactly the colour of a nutmeg ; his
hair was thick but not bushy, and he wore
it gathered up into a tuft over either ear,
in much the same manner as was fashion-
able at the French Court in the year 1671.

In spite of his convert's advantageous
appearance and easy manners Mr. Fortune
judged that he was not the child of any
one particularly rich or distinguished ; for
in these islands where the poorest are scrupu-
lously clean and the richest may wear for

22

sole adornment the sophisticated elegance of freshly gathered flowers, social standing may yet be deduced from the degree of tattooing. Lueli had greaves and gaiters of a pattern of interlacing bamboo-shoots, and in addition a bracelet round his left wrist and on his right shoulder-blade an amusing sprig. But this was all. And from the elegance of the designs and their wilful disposition it seemed as though he had been decorated for no better reason than the artist's pleasure.

When Mr. Fortune came to make inquiries he found that he had judged rightly. Lueli was one of a large family, which is rare in these islands. His mother was a fat, giggling creature, without a care in the world ; even among the light-hearted people of Fanua she and her brood were a byword for their harum-scarum ways. Their dwelling was a big tumble-down hut in which there was scarcely ever any one at home except a baby ; and though they had no apparent father or other means of sustenance, that was no obstacle to well-being in this fertile spot where no one need go hungry who could shake fruit off a tree or pull fish out of the water.

All of the family were popular. Lueli in

particular for his beauty and amiability was a regular village pet. But, whether it be that an uncommon share of good looks, like a strain of fairy blood, sets their owners apart, or whether beautiful people are in some way aware of the firebrand they carry with them and so are inclined to solitariness, Lueli, like other beauties, had for all his affability a tincture of aloofness in his character. Although he was a pet, it was not a pet dog he resembled, solicitous and dependent, but a pet cat, which will leap on to a knee to be fondled and then in a moment detach itself, impossible to constrain as a beam of moonlight playing bo-peep through a cloud. So when he deserted the village and attached himself to the newcomer no one was hurt or surprised, they took it for granted that he would go where he pleased.

This complaisance had slightly shocked Mr. Fortune, particularly as it fell in so conveniently for his wishes. It was most desirable, indeed almost necessary, that his convert should live with him, at any rate for the present, in order to assure and perfect the work of conversion. Afterwards the finished product could be let loose again, a holy decoy, to lure others into salvation's net.

But good men do not expect silver spoons to be slipped into their mouths. Easy fortune finds them unprepared and a trifle suspicious.

Mr. Fortune sought to inoculate his good luck by a scrupulous observance of formalities. He put on his black felt hat and went to pay a call on Lueli's mother. On the fourth visit he happened to find her at home. Taking off the hat and bowing, he addressed her with a long speech in which he drew a careful distinction between obedience to God and obedience to lawful authority. Lueli, said he, having become a Christian, any attempts on her part to discourage him would be tempting Lueli to disobey God, therefore as God's priest it would be his duty to oppose them. On the other hand, as Lueli's only visible parent and lawful guardian she had an absolute right to decide whether Lueli should remain at home, and if she wished him (Lueli) to do so, far from opposing her he (Mr. Fortune) would enforce her authority with his own and insist upon the boy's return.

Lueli's mother looked rather baffled, and crumpled her face exactly as Lueli crumpled his in the effort to follow Mr. Fortune's explanation. But when he had finished she brightened, said that it was all a very good scheme, and asked if Mr. Fortune would like a netful of shrimps?

He spoke a little longer of his affection for the boy, and his plans for teaching him, explaining that though perhaps an European education might not be much use in Fanua, wherefore he was not proposing to trouble him with much arithmetic, yet a Christian education is useful anywhere, and so Lueli must soon learn the Catechism; and then carrying the shrimps he set off to visit Ori.

Ori was the chief man of the island and it would be only civil and politic to consult him. Besides, there was always the chance that Ori might put a spoke in his wheel, a chance not to be missed by any conscientious Englishman. But when Ori had listened to the speech about obedience to God and obedience to lawful authority which Mr. Fortune delivered all over again (with, of course, suitable omissions and alterations) he also said that it was all a very good scheme. Wouldn't Mr. Fortune like a girl too?

Mr. Fortune refused, as politely as his horror would allow, for he had had more than enough of the girls of Fanua. He wished them no harm, it was his hope to live in charity with all men, girls included, and he had no doubt that when they were converted they would become as much better as they should be. But in their present state they were almost beyond bearing. Once upon a time when he was still a bank clerk and had leisure for literature the phrase ' a bevy of young girls ' had sounded in his ears quite pleasantly, suggesting something soft as ' a covey of partridges ' but lighter in colour. Now it sounded like a cross between a ' pack of wolves,' ' a swarm of mosquitoes,' and ' a horde of Tartars.'

The girls of Fanua always went about in bevies, and ever since his arrival they had pestered him with their attentions. He had but to put his nose into the village for a score of brown minxes to gather round him, entangling him in garlands and snatching at his hat. If he walked on the beach at sunset repeating to himself that sonnet of Wordsworth's :

It is a beauteous evening, calm and free,
The holy time is quiet as a Nun
Breathless with adoration ; the broad sun
Is sinking down in its tranquillity ;
The gentleness of heaven is on the sea :

27

long before he had got to :

Dear Child ! dear Girl ! that walkest with
   me here,

he was sure to be interrupted by sounds of
laughter and splashing, and to find himself
encompassed by yet another bevy, naked
from the sea, and begging and cajoling him
to go bathing with them.

If he fled to the woods they followed him,
creeping softly in his tracks. When he
thought himself safe and sat down to rest
a head and shoulders would be thrust
through the greenery ; soon there would be
half a dozen of them watching him, com-
menting and surmising on his person, and
egging each other on to approach nearer.
If he got up to walk away they burst out
after him and taking hands entrapped him
in the centre of a dance wanton enough to
inflame a maypole.

Once these nymphs surprised him bathing.
Fortunately the pool he was in was only
large enough to hold one at a time, so while
it continued to hold him he was tolerably
safe. But it was tiresome to have them
sitting all round gazing at him as though
he might shortly turn into a satyr. He told
them to go away, he even begged them to

do so, for the water was cold and as modesty compelled him to sit with as much of his person in the water as possible he was growing cramped. But all was in vain ; they sat there as expectant as a congregation, and for once sat in silence. His zeal told him that, tiresome as it all was, this opportunity for proselytising should not be missed. Accordingly he began to preach to them with chattering teeth, only his shoulders appearing above the surface of the water, draped in a sort of ruff or boa of water-weed. He preached for an hour and twenty minutes, and then, seeing that they would neither be converted nor go, he reared up out of the pool, strode over the shoulder of the nearest girl and proceeded (the word is more dignified than walked), blue and indignant, toward his clothes. Thank Heaven the young whores had not noticed them !

The best thing that could be said for the girls of Fanua (unless judged as trials of temper, mortifications, and potential stumbling-blocks, in which case they would have received very high marks) was that they afforded an admirable foil to Lueli's maidenly demeanour. Day by day he unrolled such a display of the Christian virtues, was so gentle, so biddable, so deft to oblige, so willing to learn, and just sufficiently stupid to be no trouble, that Mr. Fortune felt that he could have endured even twice as many girls as the price of being soothed by one such boy. He had never beheld, he had never dreamed of such a conversion. Indeed, if it had been his own work he would have been uneasy, wondering if it were not too good to be true. But he acknowledged it to be the Lord's doing and so he was prepared for anything.

But he was not prepared for his paragon to disappear without a word of warning and stay away for three days and four nights.

For the first twenty-four hours he thought little or nothing of it : Lueli was gone birding or gone fishing : he was playing with his friends in the village, or he might be on a visit to his mother. Mr. Fortune had no objection. On the contrary, he was rather pleased that the convert should thus hie him back to the company of his old acquaintance. There had been something disquieting, almost repulsive, in the calm way Lueli had given his former life the go-by. He would not like to think him lacking in natural affection. So he slept through the first night and dabbled through the first day without feeling any uneasiness ; but on the second night he dreamed that Lueli had come back, and waking from his dream he ran out into the dell to see if it were a true one.

There was no one there. He called—at first loudly, then he thought that Lueli might be hiding in the bushes afraid to come out lest he should be angry, so he called softly. Then he sat down in the verandah, for he knew there would be no more sleep for him that night, and began to worry, imagining all the dreadful things that might have befallen the boy, and reproaching himself bitterly for having allowed so much time to slip by before he awoke to the possibility of danger. Perhaps Lueli had been drowned. Mr. Fortune knew that he could swim like a fish, but he thought of drowning none the less. Perhaps running through the woods he had been caught like Absalom, or perhaps he had broken his leg and now, tired of calling for help, was lying snuffling with his face to the wet ground. Perhaps he had been carried off in a canoe by natives from some other island to serve as a slave or even as a meal.

'This is nonsense,' said Mr. Fortune.
'The boy is probably somewhere in the
village. I will go down as soon as it is day
and inquire for him. Only when I know
for certain that he is not there will I allow
myself to worry.'

For all that he continued to sit on the
verandah, shredding his mind into surmises
and waiting for the colour of day to come
back to the whispering bushes and the black
mountain. 'In a little while,' he thought,
'the moon will be in her first quarter and
Lueli will not be able to see his way back
if he comes by night.'

As soon as he decently could (for he had
his dignity as a missionary to keep up) he
walked to the village and made inquiries.
No one had seen Lueli; and what was
worse, no one could be persuaded into
making any suggestions as to his whereabouts or being in the least helpful. There
was some sort of feast toward; people were
hurrying from house to house with baskets and
packages, and the air was thick with taboos.
Mr. Fortune hung about for a while, but no
one encouraged him to hang on them. Presently he returned to the hut, feeling that the
Fanuans were all very heathen and hateful.

Anxious and exasperated he spent the greater part of the day roaming about the woods, harking back every hour or so to the dell and the bathing-pool on the chance that Lueli might have reappeared. In the dell the shadows moved round from west to east and the tide brimmed and retrenched the pool ; everything seemed to be in a conspiracy to go on as usual. By sunset he had tormented himself out of all self-control. His distress alternated with gusts of furious anger against his convert. Blow hot, blow cold, each contrary blast fanned his burning. At one moment he pictured Lueli struggling in the hands of marauding cannibals : in the next he was ready to cast him off (that is if he came back) as a runagate, and he began to prepare the scathing and renouncing remarks which should dismiss him. 'Not that I am angry,' he assured himself. ' I am not in the least angry. I am perfectly cool. But I see clearly that this is the end. I have been deceived in him, that is all. Of course I am sorry. And I shall miss him. He had pretty ways. He seemed so full of promise.'

And instantly he was ravaged with pity for the best and most ill-prized convert the world had ever seen, and now, perhaps, the world saw him no longer. Even if he had run away and was still frolicking about at his own sweet will, there was every excuse to be made for him. He was young, he was ignorant, he had not a notion how much suffering this little escapade had entailed on his pastor, he belonged to a people to whom liberty is the most natural thing in the world. And anyhow, had he not a perfect right to run away if he chose to ? ' Good heavens, do I want him tethered to me by a string ? ' So his passion whisked him round again, and he was angrier than ever with Lueli because he was also angry with himself for being ridden by what was little better than an infatuation, unworthy of a man and far more unworthy of a missionary, whose calling it is to love all God's children equally, be they legitimated or no. And he remembered uneasily how in visiting the village that morning he had not breathed a word of conversion.

The idea of having to worry about his own conduct as well as Lueli's agitated him so extremely that he fell on his knees and took refuge in prayer, imploring that his deficiencies might be overlooked and that his sins might not be visited upon Lueli ; for it was no fault of the child's, he began to point out to the All-Knowing, that his pastor had chosen to erect him into a stumbling-block. But he was in too much of an upset to pray with any satisfaction, and finding that he was only case-making like a hired barrister he opened his Prayer Book and set himself to read the Forms of Prayer to be Used by Those at Sea, for these seemed appropriate to his case. Thence he read on through the Form and Manner of Making, Ordaining, and Consecrating of Bishops, Priests, and Deacons, and had persevered into the Accession Service when there was a noise behind him. He leapt up to welcome the truant. But it was only a stray pig, looking curiously in on him from the doorway.

' O pig ! ' Mr. Fortune exclaimed, ready just then to disburden himself to anybody. But the emotion betrayed in his hurt voice was so overwhelming that the pig turned tail and bolted.

He addressed himself once more to the Accession Service. The Prayer Book lay face downward, something had fallen out of it and lay face downward too. It was a little old-fashioned picture with a lace-paper frame, one of those holy valentines that lurk in pious Prayer Books, and in course of time grow very foxed. He looked at it. It was a print of the Good Shepherd, who with His crook was helping a lost sheep out of a pit. Careless of His own equilibrium, the Good Shepherd leant over the verge of the rocks, trying to get a firm grip on the sheep's neck and so haul him up into safety.

Smitten to the heart and feeling extremely small, Mr. Fortune closed up the print in the Prayer Book. He had a shrewd suspicion that this incident was intended as a slightly sarcastic comment on his inadequacies as a shepherd. But he took comfort too, for he felt that God had looked on his distress, even though it were with a frown. And all night (for he lay awake till dawn) he held on to this thought and endeavoured to wait still.

Having been so tossed up and down, by the morrow he was incapable of feeling anything much. He spent the day in a kind of stoical industry, visiting the islanders and preaching to them, though they heard him with even less acceptance than usual, for they were all engaged in sleeping off the feast. During the afternoon he washed his clothes and cleaned the hut, and in the evening he practised the harmonium till his back smouldered with fatigue ; and all night he lay in a heavy uncomfortable sleep, imprisoned in it, as though he were cased up in an ill-fitting leaden armour.

He awoke stupefied to bright daylight. He could scarcely remember where he was, or who he was, and his perplexity was increased by finding a number of presences, cold, sleek, and curved, disposed about his limbs. Serpents ! In a panic that was half nightmare he sat up. His bed was full of bananas, neatly arranged to encircle him as sausages are arranged to encircle a Christmas turkey. Who had put bananas in his bed ? Could it be—— ? He went swiftly and silently to the door and peered into the dell. There by the spring sat Lueli, arranging shells round the water's edge as though he were laying out a garden. His back was turned, he was so absorbed in his game that he did not discover that he was being watched. Presently he rolled over and lay on his stomach, gently kicking his heels in the air.

Mr. Fortune had a good stare at him.

Then he tiptoed back again and began to dress.

As a rule Mr. Fortune was rather careless about his appearance, and compared to the islanders he was decidedly dirty, for whereas they would bathe themselves three times a day or more, he considered that once was enough. But now he made his toilet with extraordinary circumspection and deliberation. He shaved himself as minutely as though he were about to attend an archidiaconal meeting, he parted his hair, he fastened every button with a twitch, he pulled his coat forward so that it should sit well on his shoulders, he wound up his watch and knotted his bootlaces so that they should not come undone. He even put on a hat.

All the while he had a curious sensation that he was dressing a man of stone that must needs be dressed like a dummy, for of itself it was senseless and immovable. Yet *he* was the man of stone, his fingers that slowly and firmly pushed the buttons through the button-holes and knotted the bootlaces were so remorselessly and stonily strong that if he had not been managing them with such care they would have ground the buttons to powder; and if he had allowed them for one moment to tremble the bootlaces would have snapped off in his grasp like black cotton threads.

Walking terribly and softly, and still in this curious stony dream, he stepped into the dell and advanced on Lueli. Lueli turned round. It seemed to Mr. Fortune that he was looking frightened, but he could not be sure of this for his eyes also were partaking of the nature of stone, they did not see very clearly. He came up to Lueli and took hold of him by the shoulder and jerked him on to his feet.

Then, still holding fast to Lueli's shoulder, he said :

' Where have you been ? '

Lueli said : ' I have been fishing with my two cousins. For three days we went in our boats and at night we sang.'

But Mr. Fortune did not seem to have heard him, and said again :

' Where have you been ? '

Lueli said : ' We paddled round this island and away to the north-west to an islet of shells. I have brought you back these—look !—as a present.'

For the third time Mr. Fortune asked :

' Where have you been ? '

But this time he did not wait for an answer. Putting his face close to Lueli's and speaking with his eyes shut and in a low, secret voice, he began to scold him.

' Don't tell me where you 've been. I don't care. Why should I care where you go ? You made off without asking my leave, so what is it to me where you go to or how long you stay away ? Nothing ! For I cannot allow myself to love a boy who flouts me. While you were good I loved you, but that goodness didn't last long and I don't suppose it meant much. Why did you run away ? If you had told me, if you had asked my leave, I would have given it gladly. But of course you didn't, you went off without a word, and left me to worry myself half out of my mind. Not that I worried for long. I soon saw that you didn't care a snap of your fingers for me. If you were sorry I would forgive you, but you are not sorry, you are only frightened. I am very angry with you, Lueli—for I cannot call you Theodore now.'

Mr. Fortune's eyes were shut, but he knew that Lueli was frightened for he could feel him trembling. After a minute he began again :

' I can feel how you tremble, but that is silly of you, it only shows how little you understand me. You have no reason to be frightened, don't think I would punish you with blows for I would never do such a thing, I don't approve of it. But something I must do. I must tell you when you do wrong, for it seems that you yourself don't know the difference between good and bad. Why did you run away without telling me where you were going ? Was that like a Christian ? Was that like a child of God ? Do you suppose Samuel would have behaved so, whom you pretend to take such an interest in ? '

Mr. Fortune had almost talked himself out. He was feeling dazed by the sound of his own voice, sounding so different too, and he wished Lueli would take a turn. But Lueli continued to tremble in silence, he did not even wriggle, so Mr. Fortune exerted himself to say a few last words.

' Come now, Lueli, what is it to be ? Don't be frightened of me. I mean you nothing but good. Perhaps I spoke too angrily, if so, you must forgive me. I was wrong to scold ; but you really are maddening, and I have been very anxious about you and not slept much since you ran away. Anxiety always makes people seem stern.'

Now he spoke almost pleadingly, but he still had his hand fast on Lueli's shoulder. At length he noticed this, for his hand was no longer stone but flesh and blood which ached from the intensity of its grip. He withdrew it, and in an instant Lueli had ducked sideways, and with a spring like a frightened deer he fled into the bushes.

Mr. Fortune was in a state to do anything that was desperate, though what, he had not the slightest idea. But suddenly, and completely to his surprise, he found himself convulsed with laughter. He did not know what he was laughing at, till in a flash he remembered Lueli's bolt for safety, and the ludicrous expression, half abject, half triumphantly cunning, with which he had made off. To run away again when he was in such disgrace for running away— this stroke, so utterly unexpected, so perfectly natural, rapt him into an ecstasy of appreciation. He forgave everything that had gone before for leading up to this. And the brat had done it so perfectly too. If he had practised nothing else for years he could not have surpassed that adroit, terror-stricken bound, nor the glance he cast over his shoulder—deprecating, defiant, derisive, alive.

He had never been so real before.

Mr. Fortune propped himself against a tree and laughed himself weak. He had laughed his hat off, his ribs ached, and he squealed as he fetched his breath. At last he could laugh no more. He slid to the ground and lay staring up into the branches with a happy and unseeing interest. He was looking at his thoughts : thoughts that at a less fortunate juncture might have pained him but that now seemed as remote and impersonal a subject for consideration as the sway and lapse of the fronds moving overhead.

How near he had gone to making an irremediable fool of himself, and perhaps worse than a fool ! This came of letting oneself get into a fuss, of conscientiously supposing oneself to be the centre of the universe. A man turned into stone by a fury of self-justification, he had laid hold of Lueli and threatened him with pious wrath whilst all the time his longing had been to thrash the boy or to smite his body down on the grass and ravish it. Murder or lust,

43

it had seemed that only by one or the other could he avenge his wounded pride, the priestly rage against the relapsed heretic. And then by the grace of God Lueli had leapt aside with that ludicrous expression, that fantastic agility : and by a moment's vivid realisation of his convert's personality, of Lueli no longer a convert but a person, individual, unexpected, separate, he was released, and laughed the man of stone away.

He looked back on it without embarrassment or any feelings of remorse. Remorse was beside the point for what was so absolutely over and done with. Lueli had nothing to fear from him now—unless it were indigestion ; for he proposed to make him some coco-nut buns as a peace-offering. They were quite easy to make. One just grated the coco-nut into a bowl, added a little water, and drove the contents round with a spoon till they mixed. Then one formed the mixture into rocks, made each rock into a package with leaves, and baked them under the ashes. The results were quite palatable while they remained hot. And Lueli would take it as a compliment.

He would set about it presently. Meanwhile he would lie here, looking up at the tree and taking an interest in his sensations. ' I suppose it is partly reaction,' he thought, ' but I do feel most extraordinarily happy. And as mild as milk—as mothers' milk.' He was not only happy, he was profoundly satisfied, and rather pleased with himself, with his new self, that is.

' And why shouldn't I be ? It is a great improvement on the old. It would be absurd to pretend now that I am not entirely different to what I was then. I might as well refuse to feel pleased at waking from a nightmare. A nightmare, a storm of error. The heavens after a thunder-storm, and the air, are so radiant, so fresh, that they seem to be newly created. But they are not : the heavens and the eternal air were created once for all, it is only in man, that creature of a day, so ignorant and fugitive, that these changes can be wrought. The great thing, though, is not to make too much fuss about it. One should take things as they come, and keep reasonably busy. Those buns . . . How I must have frightened that pig ! '

This time there were no bananas round him when he woke, and no sign of Lueli. He did not fret himself ; knowing how very unfrightening he was he could not seriously apprehend that his convert was much frightened of him.

Nor was he. For hearing his name called he came out from where he had been reconnoitring in the bushes with scufflings so soft and yet so persistent that they might have been self-commendatory : serene, perfectly at his ease, with a pleasant smile and his head only slightly to one side. He showed no tactless anxiety to sound himself in Mr. Fortune's good graces. Only when Mr. Fortune ventured on a few words of apology did he seem at a loss, frowning a little, and wriggling his toes. He made no answer, and presently introduced a new topic. But he made it quite sufficiently clear that he would prefer an act of oblivion.

From that day the two friends lived together in the greatest amity. True, the very next week Lueli disappeared again. But this time Mr. Fortune remembered his psalm and waited with the utmost peacefulness and contentment. Indeed he found himself quite pleased to be left to the enjoyment of his own society. It had never seemed very enjoyable in old days but it was now. For on this enchanting island where everything was so gay, novel, and forthcoming, his transplanted soul had struck root enough to be responding to the favouring soil and sending up blossoms well worth inspection.

Beyond a few romantic fancies about bathing by moonlight and a great many good resolutions to keep regular hours, Mr. Fortune had scarcely propounded to himself how he would be suited by the life of the only white man on the island of Fanua. In the stress of preparation there had been no incitement to picture himself at leisure. It seemed that between converting the islanders and dissolving soup-squares he would scarcely have an unoccupied minute. Now he found himself in possession of a great many—hours, whole days sometimes, without any particular obligation, stretching out around him waste and tranquil as the outstretched blue sky and sparkling waves.

Leisure can be a lonely thing ; and the sense of loneliness is terrifically enhanced by unfamiliar surroundings. Some men in Mr. Fortune's position might have been driven mad ; and their madness would have been all the more deep and irrevocable because the conditions that nursed it were

so paradisal. A delightful climate ; a fruit-
ful soil ; scenery of extreme and fairy-tale
beauty ; agreeable meals to be had at the
minimum of trouble ; no venomous reptiles
and even the mosquitoes not really trouble-
some ; friendly natives and the most
romantic lotus—these, and the prospect of
always these, would have mocked them into
a melancholy frenzy.

But Mr. Fortune happened to be peculiarly
well fitted to live on the island of Fanua.
Till now there had been no leisure in his
life, there had only been holidays ; and
without being aware of it, in body and soul
he was all clenched up with fatigue, so that
it was an intuitive ecstasy to relax. He
could not have put a name to the strange
new pleasure which was come into his existence. He supposed it was something in
the air.

As it was with leisure, so it was with
luxuriance. Most Englishmen who visit the
South Sea Islands are in the depths of their
hearts a little shocked at the vegetation.
Such fecundity, such a largesse and explosion
of life—trees waving with ferns, dripping
with creepers, and as it were flaunting their
vicious and exquisite parasites ; fruits like

48

an emperor's baubles, flowers triumphantly gaudy or tricked out with the most sophisticated improbabilities of form and patterning : all this profusion unbridled and untoiled for and running to waste disturbs them. They look on it as on some conflagration, and feel that they ought to turn the hose on it. Mr. Fortune was untroubled by any such thoughts, because he was humble. The reckless expenditure of God's glory did not strike him as reckless, and his admiration of the bonfire was never overcast by a feeling that he ought to do something about it. Indeed, the man who ten years ago had been putting down in Mr. Beaumont's pass-book : Orchid Growers, Ltd., £72, 15s. od., had presently ceased to pay any special attention to the vegetables of Fanua, and was walking about among them as though they were the most natural thing in the world ; which, if one comes to reflect on it, in that part of the world they were.

But though he came to disregard the island vegetation he never ceased to be attentive to the heavens. To have time to watch a cloud was perhaps the thing he was most grateful for among all his leisurely joys.

About a mile or so from the hut was a small grassy promontory, and here he would lie for hours on end, observing the skies. Sometimes he chose out one particular cloud and followed it through all its changes, watching how almost imperceptibly it amassed and reared up its great rounded cauliflower curves, and how when it seemed most proud and sculptural it began to dissolve and pour itself into new moulds, changing and changing, so that he scarcely had time to grasp one transformation before another followed it. On some days the clouds scarcely moved at all, but remained poised like vast swans floating asleep with their heads tucked under their wings. They rested on the air, and when they brightened, or changed their white plumage to the shadowy pallor of swans at dusk, it was because of the sun's slow movement, not their own. But those days came seldom, for as a rule the sea wind blew, buoying them onward.

Lying on his stomach Mr. Fortune would watch a cloud come up from the horizon, and as it approached he would feel almost afraid at the silent oncoming of this enormous and towering being, an advance

silent as the advance of its vast shadow on
the sea. The shadow touched him, it had
set foot on the island. And turning on his
back he looked up into the cloud, and
glancing inland saw how the shadow was
already climbing the mountain side.

Though they were silent he imagined then
a voice, an enormous soft murmur, sinking
and swelling as they tumbled and dissolved
and amassed. And when he went home he
noted in his diary the direction of the wind
and any peculiarities of weather that he had
noticed. At these times he often wished,
and deeply, that he had a barometer : but
he had never been able to afford himself
one, and naturally the people of the Mission
had thought of a teapot.

On the first really wet day however, he
rushed out with joy and contrived a rain-
gauge. And having settled this in and
buttered its paws, he went for a long rejoicing walk, a walk full of the most complicated animal ecstasy, or perhaps vegetable
would be the truer word ; for all round
him he heard the noise of the woods guzzling
rain, and he felt a violent sympathy with
all the greenery that seemed to be wearing
the deepened colour of intense gratification,

and with the rich earth trodden by the rain
and sending up a steam of mist as though
in acknowledgment. And all the time as
he trudged along he was pretending to
himself how hardy he was to be out in such
disagreeable weather, and looking forward
to how nice it would be to get back to the
hut and change into dry clothes and boil
a kettle for tea.

He was behaving as though he had never
been out in the rain before. It had rained
quite often in St. Fabien, indeed there were
times when it seemed never to do anything
else. But rain there had been a very
different matter, veiling the melancholy
quayside, clanking on the roofs of the rabble
of tin church premises, and churning the
soft grit of the roads into mud. It had
rained in St. Fabien and he had constantly
been out in it, but with no more ecstasy
than he had known when it rained in
Hornsey. No doubt the ownership of a
rain-gauge accounted for much ; but there
was more to it than that—a secret core of
delight, a sense of truancy, of freedom, because now for the first time in his life he
was walking in the rain entirely of his
own accord, and not because it was his

duty, or what public opinion conceived to
be so.

Public opinion was waiting for him in the
hut when he got back. While he was still
shaking himself like a dog in the verandah,
Lueli appeared in the doorway, looking very
dry and demure, and began to pet and
expostulate in the same breath.

' How very wet ! How very silly ! Come
in at once ! Why do you go out when it
rains ? '

' It is healthy to go for a walk in the
rain,' replied Mr. Fortune, trampling firmly
on public opinion.

' It would be better to stay under a roof
and sleep.'

' Not at all. In England it rains for days
at a time, but every one goes out just the
same. We should think it very effeminate
to stop indoors and sleep.'

' I haven't been asleep the whole time,'
Lueli remarked in a defensive voice. ' That
new pot of yours—I 've been out to fetch it
in case it got spoilt.'

While he was drinking his tea (Lueli
drank tea also, because his affection and
pride made him in everything a copy-cat,
but he sipped it with a dubious and wary

expression), Mr. Fortune found himself thinking of England. He thought about his father, a sanguine man who suddenly upped and shot himself through the head ; and thence his thoughts jumped to a Whitsuntide bank holiday which he had spent in a field near Ruislip. The sky was a pale milky blue, the field was edged with some dowdy elms and beyond them was a view of distant gasworks. At two o'clock he had eaten his lunch—a cold pork chop ; and clear as ever he could recall the exquisite unmeaning felicity of that moment.

How little pleasure his youth had known, that this outing should remain with him like an engraved gem ! And now he scarcely knew himself for happiness. The former things were passed away : the bank with its façade trimmed with slabs of rusticated stone—a sort of mural tripe ; his bed-sitting-room at ' Marmion,' 239 Lyttleton Road, N.E., so encumbered and subfusc ; and the horrible disappointment of St. Fabien. There had passed the worst days of his life ; for he had expected something of them, he had gone there with an intention of happiness and doing good. But though he had tried his best he had not been able to love the converts, they were degenerate, sickly, and servile ; and in his discouragement he had thought to himself : ' It 's a good thing I know about book-keeping, for I shall never be fit to do anything better.' And now he was at Fanua, and at his side squatted Lueli, carving a pattern on the rain-gauge.

The next day it rained again, and he went for another walk, a walk not so ecstatic as the former, but quite as wet and no doubt quite as healthy. Hollow peals of thunder rumbled through the cold glades, the chilling South wind blew and the coco-nuts fell thumping from the trees. He walked to his promontory and stood for some time watching the clouds—which were to-day rounded, dark, and voluminous, a presentation to the eye of what the thunder was to the ear— and the waves. He felt no love for the sea, but he respected it. That evening the rain-gauge recorded 1.24.

The project of bathing by moonlight never came to much, for somehow when the time came he was always too sleepy to be bothered ; but he was extremely successful in keeping regular hours, for all that so many of them were hours of idleness.

Morning prayers, of course, began the day, and after prayers came breakfast. A good breakfast is the foundation of a good day. Mr. Fortune supposed that a great deal of the islanders' lack of steadfastness might be attributed to their ignorance of this maxim. Lueli, for instance, was perfectly content to have no breakfast at all, or satisfied himself with a flibberty-gibberty meal of fruit eaten off the bushes. Mr. Fortune made tea, softened and sweetened at once by coco-milk, and on Sundays coffee. With this he had three boiled eggs. The eggs were those of the wild pigeon, eggs so small that three were really a quite moderate allowance. Unfortunately there was no certainty of them being new-laid, and very often they were not. So it was a notable day when it occurred to him that a native dish of bread-fruit sopped into a paste was sufficiently stodgy and sticky to be perfectly well eaten in lieu of porridge.

After breakfast and a pipe shared with Lueli—he did not really approve of boys of Lueli's years smoking, but he knew that pipe-sharing was such an established Polynesian civility that Lueli's feelings would be seriously wounded if he didn't fall in with the custom—the hut was tidied, the mats shaken in the sun, and the breakfast things put away. Then came instruction in befitting branches of Christian lore ; then, because the pupil was at hand and it was well to make sure of him while he had him. For all that there were a good many holidays given and taken. With such an admirable pupil he could afford himself the pleasures of approbation.

Since the teaching had to be entirely conversational, Lueli learnt much that was various and seemingly irrelevant. Strange alleys branched off from the subject in hand, references and similes that strayed into the teacher's discourse as the most natural things in the world had to be explained and enlarged upon. In the middle of an account of Christ's entry into Jerusalem Mr. Fortune would find himself obliged to break off and describe a donkey. This would lead naturally to the sands of Weston-super-Mare, and a short account of bathing-machines ; and that afternoon he would take his pupil down to the beach and show him how English children turned sand out of buckets, and built castles with a moat round them. Moats might lead to the Feudal System and the Wars of the Barons. Fighting Lueli understood very well, but other aspects of civilisation needed a great deal of explaining ; and Mr. Fortune nearly gave himself heat apoplexy by demonstrating in the course of one morning the technique of urging a golf ball out of a bunker and how English housewives crawl about on their hands and knees scrubbing the linoleum.

After dismissing Lueli from his lessons Mr. Fortune generally strolled down to the village to enlarge the work of conversion. By now he had given up general preaching and exhortation—not that he thought it a bad way to go to work, on the contrary, he knew that it had been sanctioned by the best Apostolic usage ; but preaching demands the concurrence of an audience, even though it be one of fishes or pigs ; and since he was no longer a novelty the islanders had become as slippery as the one, as artful and determined in dodging away as the other. He practised instead the Socratic method of pouncing upon any solitary and defenceless person who happened to pass by. And like Socrates he would lead them aside into the shade and ask them questions. Many charming conversations took place.

But nothing ever came of them, and the fields so white for the harvest continued to ripple and rustle in the sun, eluding all his efforts to reap and bind them into sheaves and carry them into God's barn in time for the harvest-home.

He had now been on the island for nearly six months, and every day he knew himself to have less attractive power. How he wished that he had thought of bringing some fireworks with him ! Two or three rockets touched off, a green Bengal light or a Catherine wheel, he would have been sure of a congregation then. And there is no religious reason why fireworks should not be used as a means to conversion. Did not God allure the fainting Israelites by letting Himself off as a pillar of fire by night? He thought, though, that had he fireworks at his command he would draw the line at that variety which is known as British Cannon. They are very effective, but they are dangerous ; and he did not wish to frighten his flock.

From midday till about two or three in the afternoon there was no possibility of converting anybody, for the islanders one and all went firmly to sleep. This was the time when Mr. Fortune went for his daily walk. After so much endeavour he would have been quite pleased to take a nap himself ; but he knew the value of regular exercise, and by taking it at this time of day he was safe from molestation by the bevies. He usually ate a good deal of fruit on these walks, because he had not yet accustomed himself to such a long stretch between breakfast and dinner. Indeed for some time after his arrival on the island he felt rather underfed. Dinner consisted of more bread-fruit, messes prepared by Lueli, fish sometimes, roots flavoured with sea-water. Lueli preferred his fish raw. Sometimes Mr. Fortune made soup or opened a tin of sardines.

Dinner was immediately followed by afternoon tea. Mr. Fortune would not forego that comfortable meal, so they had it as a sort of dessert. Then followed a long sub-afternoon, spent in various ways of doing nothing in particular. Lueli always went bathing then. He had no theories about it being dangerous to bathe on the heels of a large meal, and after an interval for digestion Mr. Fortune bathed too. Sometimes they paid visits, or received them.

On these occasions Mr. Fortune never spoke of religion. He produced his pocket magnifying-glass and showed them his pores. At other times they went sailing or took a stroll.

These were all pleasant doings, but perhaps the moment he enjoyed best was when, dusk having fallen, he lit the lamp. He had a peculiar affection for his lamp. It hung from the ridge-pole of the hut, and he felt about it much as Sappho felt about the evening star. It shone as though with a kindness upon everything that was dear to him : upon his books and the harmonium; upon the bowls and dishes and woven mats that were both dear in themselves as tokens of the islanders' good-will, and endeared by use ; upon the wakeful shine of the teapot and the black tin box, and upon Lueli's sleepy head. He would often walk out into the darkness for the pleasure of seeing his hut lighted up within, the rays of warm light shining through the chinks in the latticed walls as though they were shining through a very large birds' nest. Overhead were the stars trembling with the intensity of their remote fires. The air was very sweet and the dark grass gentle underfoot as he walked round about his home.

He whistled to himself, softly, an air that Delilah sings in the oratorio of *Samson*—a rather foolish, chirruping tune, in which Handel expressed his private opinion of soprano Delilahs : but he liked the words—

How charming is domestic ease,
A thousand ways I 'll strive to please :

(after that they ceased to be appropriate).

A thousand, thousand ways he would strive to please until he had converted all the islanders. And planning new holy wiles for the morrow, he re-entered the hut to eat a slight supper, and perhaps to darn a rent or replace a button, and then to write up his diary, to read prayers, and so to end another day.

Saturdays and Saints' days were holidays, for himself and Lueli both. Lueli disported himself as he pleased, and Mr. Fortune watched clouds. On Sundays they performed the services appointed by the Church of England.

There was a week or two when he believed that he was in the way to make another convert. She was a very old woman, extremely ugly, not very agreeable, and rather doting. But she seemed perfectly

able to understand about eternal life, and
showed great anxiety to lay hold on it.
Mr. Fortune visited her daily and tried hard
to teach her the love of God, and the
Christian belief. But she seemed deaf to
all topics save one—and her anxiety to lay
hold became as the days went by positively
grasping.

One day the wife of Teioa, a sensible
woman whom Mr. Fortune had a great
respect for, came in with some food for
the invalid and overheard part of their
colloquy.

' Live for ever,' she remarked rather scorn-
fully to the missionary as they left the house.
' Why, isn't she old enough already ? How
much more does she want ? ' And though
Mr. Fortune deplored her blindness, yet in
this particular instance he admitted to himself that she had perceived clearly enough,
and that his old woman was no sort of
genuine convert, only very old and frightened
and rapacious. None the less he continued
to visit her, and to do what he could to
comfort her. And often as he sat by her
bedside he thought what a mystery this
business of eternal life is, and how strangely,
though almost all desire it, they differ in

their conception of what it is they desire ; some, like Shakespeare (and how many others unknown ?) coolly confident of an immortality

> Where breath most breathes, even in the
>   mouths of men ;

some, like Buddha, hoping for an eternal life in which their own shall be absolved and lost ; some, like this old woman, desiring an eternity like an interminable piece of string which she could clutch one end of and reel for ever about herself. 'And how do I desire it ? ' he thought. ' I want to feel it on every side, more abundantly. But I want to die first.'

In the end he grew quite attached to the old creature, and when she died he was sorry. He would have liked, as a mark of respect, to attend her funeral : (he certainly did not feel that he had any claim to conduct it himself). But no one suggested that he should, and he hesitated to suggest it lest he should be offending against some taboo. So he went off by himself for a day in the woods and thought about her, and said a prayer or two. And in the evening he returned to Lueli. One convert at any rate had been granted to him, and perhaps it would be greedy to want more, especially as that one was in every way so exemplary and delightful.

The two friends—for such they were despite more than sixty degrees of latitude and over thirty years between them (and the latter is a more insuperable barrier than an equator)—lived together in the greatest amity. Lueli had now quite given up running away. He settled down to Mr. Fortune's ways, and curled himself up amidst the new customs and regulations as peacefully as though he had never known any other manner of existence. Indeed Mr. Fortune was sometimes obliged to pack him off to the village to play with the other boys, thinking that it would harm him never to be with company of his own age.

Lueli was no anchorite, he enjoyed larking about the island with his friends as much as any boy should do ; but what he loved beyond anything was novelty, and for this he worshipped Mr. Fortune, whose every action might reveal some new and august entertainment. The faces he made in shaving, the patch of hair on his chest, his ceremonious method of spitting out pips into his hand, the way in which his boot-laces went round the little hooks, his watch, his pockets and the things he kept in them—Lueli might grow accustomed to these daily delights, but he did not tire of them any more than Wordsworth tired of the Lesser Celandine. And there was more than this, and much more : prayer, the harmonium, the sewing-machine, religious instruction and occasional examples of European cookery. Prayer Lueli had taken to from the beginning, but he needed to acclimatise himself to the harmonium. When Mr. Fortune played to him he would sit as close as possible to the instrument, quivering like a dog and tilting up his chin with such an ecstatic and woebegone look that Mr. Fortune almost expected him to howl ; and thinking that he didn't really enjoy it he would leave off playing. But Lueli would then edge a little closer and beg for more, and Mr. Fortune was only too glad to comply.

Like the harpsichord, the harmonium has a repertory of its own, pieces that can only be properly rendered on this instrument. Naturally I do not speak of the harmonium compositions of such recent composers as Schoenberg or Max Reger : these would have been too difficult for Mr. Fortune to play even if they had been stocked by the music-shop he had frequented. But without being in any way a virtuoso—and some think that the harmonium, being essentially a domesticated instrument, sober and of a religious cast, is inherently unsuited for displays of skill—Mr. Fortune played quite nicely and had a repertory of many classical larghettos and loud marches, besides, of course, the usual hymns and chants. Haydn was his favourite composer ; and arrangements from the string quartets go rather well on the harmonium.

Lueli too was a musician after a simpler fashion. He had a wooden pipe, rather like a flageolet, of a small compass and a sad, squeaky tone ; and the two friends passed many happy evenings entertaining each other with their performances. First Mr. Fortune obliged, leaning forward at an acute angle on the music-stool, his knees rising and falling like parts of a machine, his face very close to the music, his large hands manœuvring among the narrow keys, or sometimes hovering like a bee in a flower border over the ranks of stops, pulling out one, hitting another back with a tap, as

though his fingers could read, though rather
short-sightedly, in black Gothic lettering on
the ivory knobs such names as Gamba,
Corno di Bassetto, Bourdon, or Dulciana.
And then, when rising he released the last
throbbing chord and stretched himself (for
he was a tall man, and in order to adjust
his body and legs to the instrument he had
to assume a rather cramped position), it
was pleasant to see Lueli discoursing music
in his turn, and a curious study in con-
trasts. For the boy sat cross-legged on the
floor, or leant against the wall in the attitude
of the boy in the statue, an attitude so
physically nonchalant, so spiritually intent,
that whoever looks at the statue, or even a
cast of it or a photograph, understands,
sometimes with a kind of jealous horror,
how musicians are free of a world of their
own, inhabiting their bodies as it were
nominally or by proxy—just as we say of a
house : That is Mr. So-and-So's ; but the
house is empty save for a sleepy caretaker,
the owner is away travelling in Africa.

Lueli's tunes were very long tunes, though
the phrases composing them were short ;
the music seemed to waver to and fro,
alighting unexpectedly and then taking

another small flight, and listening to it was like watching a bird flitting about in a bush ; the music ends, the bird flies away ; and one is equally at a loss to explain why the bird stayed so long and seemed so busy or why it suddenly made up its mind that the time had come for a longer flight, for a flight that dismisses it from our vision.

To tell the truth, Mr. Fortune was not as much impressed by Lueli's music as Lueli was by his. His chin even sank further into his chest as he sat, his listening flesh was unmoved, and he never felt the least impulse to howl. Mr. Fortune, in spite of his superior accomplishments, his cultivated taste, and enough grasp of musical theory to be able to transpose any hymn into its nearly related keys, was not so truly musical as Lueli. For instance, he never had the least idea whether Lueli's tunes were lively or sad. They all seemed alike to him. But Lueli learnt almost immediately to distinguish between a march and a sentimental piece, and as the harmonies grew more and more passionate his chin would lift higher, his mouth would contract, and the shadow of his long eyelashes would shorten up over his cheek.

It would have been pleasant if the two musicians could have joined forces. Mr. Fortune by listening very often and pretty intently to Lueli's rambling tunes was able to memorise two of them—as he believed, perfectly. Sending Lueli down to the village he spent an afternoon practising these two melodies on the harmonium and putting in a part for the left hand. It would make an agreeable surprise for his boy, he thought, to hear his tunes played by some one else; and then with Lueli playing his pipe whilst he supported the melody with chords and figurations they could achieve a duet. But the surprise fell quite flat; perhaps Mr. Fortune's European harmonies queered the pitch, perhaps he had misunderstood the time-values; in any case Lueli showed no signs of recognising the tunes, and even when their identity was pointed out to him he seemed doubtful. As for the duet plan it was not feasible, for the harmonium was tuned to the mean tone temperament and Lueli's pipe obeyed some unscientific native scale; either alone sounded all right, but in conjunction they were painfully discordant.

Finding it impossible to convert Lueli's pipe, Mr. Fortune next essayed to train his voice to Christian behaviour. In this he was more successful; Lueli's voice was of a nondescript newly broken timbre. He couldn't always control it, and Mr. Fortune had to smoke his pipe very hard in order not to laugh at the conjunction of Lueli's expression, so determined in well-doing, and the vagaries of his voice wandering from the straight path and ricochetting from note to note.

He also taught him to whistle, or tried to, for he was rather shocked at the idea of a boy not knowing how to whistle, explaining to him beforehand the secular nature of the act, and forbidding him to whistle tunes that had any especially sacred associations. But though Lueli screwed up his lips and almost burst himself taking in breath his whistling remained of a very girlish incompetent kind. On the other hand he showed an immediate aptitude for the vulgar kind of whistling which is done with a blade of grass. The first hearing of this was one of the pleasantest surprises that his pastor gave him. He mastered the technique in a few minutes and raced off to show the new accomplishment to his friends in the village. The fashion caught on like wildfire, and soon every boy on the island was looking for the proper blades of grass, which are called squeakers. The woods rang with their performances, and the parrots looked down with awe and astonishment at hearing men producing sounds so much more ear-splitting than anything they could achieve themselves.

The fashion raged like wildfire, and like wildfire burnt itself out. The groves were peaceful again, that is to say peaceful as any groves can be with parrots in them (not that the reader should suppose that the parrots at Fanua were like the parrots in the Zoological Gardens : oppression makes them much noisier) ; and every one was out in the salt-meadows, passionately flying kites.

The islanders were like that ; enthusiastic and fickle, they would wear a whim to shreds and cast it away in the course of a week. Lueli was as bad ; if it had not been for Mr. Fortune he would never have persevered in anything. It was provoking for a master to find his pupil so changeable and inconstant, all the more so because of Lueli's extraordinary docility and aptitude in learning. Nothing could have exceeded the readiness with which he accepted a new idea ; and finding him so swift to become a Christian Mr. Fortune used to wonder why the other islanders would not respond as pleasantly to his teaching, for at this time he was still in hopes of converting the whole island. He preached to them, he prayed among them, every night and morning he prayed for them, he gave them biscuits and showed them pictures. They behaved themselves to him most charmingly, tactfully overlooking his blunders in etiquette, accepting him as their friend, though an unaccountable one. But his message they would not accept, it slid off them as though their very innocence and guilelessness had spread a fine impermeable film over their souls.

' After all,' thought Mr. Fortune, ' I have not made a single convert in this island though it is now almost a year since I came. For I did not convert Lueli, God gave him to me (by the way I must remember to call him Theodore). And God still withholds the others.'

This was a comfortable point of view. It satisfied Mr. Fortune, all the more so since it agreed so aptly with his psalm, of which the last verse runs : ' And that Thou, Lord, art merciful : for Thou rewardest every man according to his work.' And he quoted this verse of it in the report which he handed to Archdeacon Mason on returning to St. Fabien to buy more stores and give an account of his ministry.

The Archdeacon frowned slightly when he laid down the report, which was a pretty piece of work, for Mr. Fortune had written it in his neatest hand and Lueli (under his direction) had tinted blue, fawn-colour, and green the little sketch-map of the island which embellished it as a frontispiece.

The next day Mr. Fortune called upon his superior. ' My dear Fortune,' said he after a few polite questions about the soil of Fanua and its marriage ceremonies, ' this is excellent ' (here he tapped the report which lay on the table). ' Indeed I may say it is idyllic. But you must allow me to make one comment, you must let me tell you that there is such a thing as being too modest. Believe me, conversions at the rate of one *per annum* are not an adequate reward of your works. God's grace is infinite, and I am sure that your labours have been most truly conscientious ; and

yet you say you have made only one convert.
This is not enough—mind, I would not speak
a word of blame. I only say—if I may so
express myself—that there must have been a
leakage somewhere, a leakage ! '

He paused. Mr. Fortune looked at his
hands and realised how sunburnt they had
become.

' Compel them to come in, you know.'

Mr. Fortune wondered if he should confess
to his superior the one so nearly disastrous
occasion when he had tried to use compul-
sion. But the Archdeacon's metaphor about
the leakage had pained him and he decided
not to. Instead he asked the Archdeacon
how he would advise him to act in order to
convert the whole island.

It was rather a shock to him to be recom-
mended to take a leaf out of the Jesuits' book.
However on the first evening of his return
to the island he began to make some discreet inquiries of Lueli about what gods
the islanders worshipped, though being very
careful to convey by his tone and choice of
words that he thought it a terrible pity that
they should not worship his.

' Oh, they,' said Lueli, offering him some
more fruit, which Mr. Fortune refused, since

he had been stuffed with gifts in kind ever since the moment he got out of the launch. ' Oh, they—they only worship one god.'

This answer did not sound quite as it should ; and in deference to his recent memories of the Archdeacon, Mr. Fortune ran his convert through the Apostles' Creed before proceeding with his inquiries. It was quite all right. Lueli remembered the creed without a single lapse, and on further questioning Mr. Fortune discovered that the islanders worshipped one god each, a much more suitable state of affairs for heathens ; although on thinking it over before he fell asleep the missionary reflected that in the island of Fanua conversion must necessarily be a slow business since he would have to break the faggot stick by stick. Just before he lost consciousness he began to wonder what sort of god Lueli had worshipped.

In the morning he remembered his curiosity. He said to Lueli : ' What god had you before I came and taught you to know the true God ? '

' I 'll show him to you,' said Lueli ; and running into the bushes he presently returned with an idol about two foot long.

Mr. Fortune looked at the idol very

seriously, almost respectfully, as though he were measuring swords with an adversary. It was a rather well-looking idol, made of wood and nicely polished, and he was pleased to note that it was not obscene ; but for all that a slight shudder ran through his flesh, such as one feels on looking at a dead snake even though one knows that it is a dead one.

'Drop it,' he commanded, and the boy laid it down on the grass between them. Mr. Fortune remembered the words of a female missionary from China who had visited St. Fabien on a tour. 'The first thing I make my converts do,' she had said, and as she spoke she clenched her hands till the knuckles showed up as bones, ' is to destroy their idols. Then I can feel sure of them. And not till then.'

Talking over her lecture afterwards Mr. Fortune had been of the opinion of the majority : that the lady missionary had been right. ' I don't agree at all,' said his friend, Henry Merton. ' We teach that idols are the works of men's hands, things of wood and stone. To insist on their destruction is to show our converts that we believe in them ourselves, that we look on them with anxiety and attribute power to them. No, no, it is silly to take any idol so seriously ! ' And Mr. Fortune, who was humble before others, thought that after all he had judged too hastily and that his friend was in the right of it.

Soon after that Henry Merton had died, and the words of the dead have a special value. Mr. Fortune remembered his friend's opinion, but he also remembered the female missionary. She had spoken with an air of authority ; and for all he knew she might be dead too, she might even be a martyr. He stood and looked at Lueli's idol which lay on the grass between them and he wondered if he should tell Lueli to burn it. At last, without saying anything, he walked into the hut. When he came out again Lueli was scouring a wooden bowl with sand and the idol was gone.

One of the Archdeacon's first questions about the convert of Fanua was : Had Mr. Fortune dressed him properly ? And Mr. Fortune had replied with perfect candour that he had been too busy caring for his soul to think of his clothing. This too the Archdeacon had objected to, saying that dress made a great difference, and that when

the other islanders saw Lueli dressed befittingly they would become aware of their
nakedness and wish to be converted and
wear white raiment.

' But they have seen me, *I* have never
omitted to dress myself since I have lived
on Fanua.'

' No, no, of course not,' answered the
Archdeacon, a little testily, for really the
missionary's simplicity was making him very
argumentative and tiresome. ' But that is
not to the point, for you surely don't suppose
that they look on you as one of themselves.
You must clothe that boy, Fortune, you
must make him wear trousers and a tunic.
And at night he must wear a night-shirt.'

So now, seeing that the idol was gone,
Mr. Fortune called Lueli into the hut and
began to measure him. He had never learnt
tailoring ; however he supposed that by
taking great care and doing his best he could
turn out a suit of clothes which might in-
sinuate the fact of their nakedness to the
islanders of Fanua, even if it had no other
merit. He measured Lueli, he wrote down
the measurements, he made his calculations
and drew a sort of ground plan. Then he
fetched a roll of white cotton and having laid

it upon the floor and tethered it with some
books he crawled about on all fours cutting
out the trousers and the tunic with a pair of
nail-scissors ; for he thought that the night-
shirt might rest in abeyance for the present.

The nail-scissors could only manage very
small bites, and by the time the cutting-out
was completed he was rather dizzy and very
hot from taking so much exercise on his
knees. 'That will do for the present,' he
thought, rolling up the pieces. 'This afternoon I will visit my parishioners. Perhaps
as they have not seen me for a week they will
be more inclined to listen to my teaching.
And I must keep my eyes open for idols.'

But early on the morrow Mr. Fortune got
out the sewing-machine and continued his
career as a tailor. The sewing-machine was
suffering from the sea-air, it needed a great
deal of oil and adjustment before it could be
got to run smoothly, but he mastered it in
the end and began to sew up the seams. As
time went on he grew more and more excited.
He worked the treadles faster and faster, he
had never, even for the most spirited march,
trodden the pedals of his harmonium so
frantically ; the machine rocked under his
zeal and all the time the needle kept darting

up and down, piercing the cotton with small accurate stabs in a way that seemed to express a kind of mechanical malevolence. The seams were all finished, the hems were turned up ; now it was evening, there was nothing left but the buttons. Those he must put on by hand.

All day Lueli had sat beside him watching his performance with rapture. It was the machine which ravished him, he was not so much interested in the clothes. But when Mr. Fortune called him in a rather solemn voice and began to dress him, holding up the tunic above his head as though it were a form of baptism, he too began to put on looks of solemnity and importance.

The tunic fitted tolerably enough though there was no elegance about it ; but alas ! the trousers were a sad blow to Mr. Fortune. For he had designed them on a two-dimensional basis, cutting out the back and the front in one operation on a doubled fold of the cloth, and forgetting that even the slimmest boy is bulkier behind than in front ; so that when attired in these unfortunate garments it was difficult for Lueli to move and almost impossible for him to sit down. He, in his innocence, thought the trousers

all that they should be, and late as it was he
wished to run down to the village in order to
wake up his friends and show them his fine
clothes. But Mr. Fortune bade him take
them off. It made his heart bleed to see his
boy made such a figure of fun, and when the
living Lueli emerged from his white cotton
sepulchre he privately called the Archdeacon a fool and forswore the idea of the
night-shirt for good and all. But on the next
day and on the next again he struggled to
make a practicable pair of trousers, and in
the end he produced a pair that were rather
on the baggy side perhaps, but still they
were tolerable.

Unfortunately by this time his convert's
ardour was somewhat quenched. He had
been measured so often, he had stood still to
be fitted when he wanted to go fishing, he
had had pins run into him, and all this had
made this particular novelty seem rather a
tedious example of his pastor's odd ways.
So though he put on his white raiment at
command and walked decorously through
the village beside Mr. Fortune to be an
object lesson, his demeanour, while admir-
ably meek and civil, wasn't much of an
advertisement for the happiness of those

who are clothed in the whole armour of God.

The Archdeacon's theory was not borne out by events. The islanders were too much struck and roused to speculation by the sight of Lueli's apparel to spare a thought for their own nakedness. At first they were of the opinion that this was some new and powerful taboo invented by the stranger. They shrank back, and averted their eyes as if from some improper spectacle. Lueli's mother was actually moved to a display of maternal feeling. She rushed weeping from the crowd, hurled herself at Mr. Fortune's knees and began to implore him not to ruin the boy's prospects. Disentangling himself a little pettishly from her pleadings, Mr. Fortune explained that clothing such as this would do Lueli nothing but good : indeed, she herself would be none the worse for something of the sort. She took him at his word ; before he could stay her she had torn the clothes off her son and was squirming into them. She was several sizes too fat, and Mr. Fortune saw his seams being rent open in all directions. He had to bribe her with a promise of the blue glass mulberries from his Christmas tree selection before she would

consent to undress. Finally he had to ease
her out himself. It was a good thing that
the Archdeacon was not present, but for all
that Mr. Fortune half wished that he had
been.

On their return he sewed up the seams
once more and called Lueli. The boy began
to protest and argue. Then he changed his
methods and started coaxing. Mr. Fortune
had his own ideas as to how Lueli should be
managed. Rising discreetly he opened the
harmonium and said that it was time to
study another hymn.

That night he lay awake, wondering what
he would do if his convert rebelled. He had
already decided to drop the Archdeacon's
tactics at the first seemly opportunity ; but
he wished to choose the opportunity and
do the dropping himself. He might have
spared himself this anxiety. On the morrow
Lueli donned the trousers and the tunic with
a very matter of course air, and half an hour
later went off to bathe. And it was a sure
thing that if formerly he had bathed twice or
thrice a day he now bathed as often again,
undressing with a bland smile and folding up
his white raiment with the utmost neatness.
Of course it was a pretext ; and the mission-

ary wondered if his charge was learning
to be deceitful. But Lueli's deceitfulness
was so very open and unconcerned that it
could scarcely be reckoned as the genuine
article.

The clothes were always deposited very
carefully in some place where they would
have every opportunity of happening to fall
into the sea. At the end of a week they were
so saturated with brine as to be quite un-
wearable. Exercising his authority, Mr. Fortune forbade Lueli to wear them any more.

Lueli would bathe anywhere, he seemed
equally happy lolling on the Pacific Ocean
or folded up in a pool the size of a bedroom
basin with a little waterfall splashing on his
head. Mr. Fortune was more ceremonious.
It was he who instituted the bathing-pool as
a regular adjunct to their life.

About half a mile from the hut and near
the cloud observatory was a small rocky cove
with a half-moon of white shell-beach and a
slope of fine sward running back into the
woods. A small rivulet debouched here,
very convenient for washing off the sea-salt
in ; and as the mouth of the cove was
guarded by a barrier of coral-reef the water
within was almost as still as a lake, and so

clear that one could look down and see the
weeds twenty feet below slowly twirling their
vast brown or madder-coloured ribbons, and
the fish darting among them.

Mr. Fortune often thought of Robinson
Crusoe and his man Friday as he sat on the
rocks watching Lueli at his interminable
diversions in the pool. Living on an island
alone with his convert, spiritually alone at
any rate, for though he had not given up
hope of the other Fanuans and still visited
them pretty frequently, he could never feel
the kinship with them which he felt so
securely with Lueli, the comparison could
scarcely fail to occur to him. And he
thought gratefully how much happier he was
than the other man. *He* was ideally contented with his island and with his companion, he had come there by his own wish,
and he liked the life so well that he proposed
to continue in it until his death. So little
did it distress him to be away from civilisation that he was of his own will paring away
the slender bonds that tied him to the rest of
the world. For after the first visit to St.
Fabien he had paid no more, and for the
last twelvemonth he had not even bestirred
himself to write a report to be sent by canoe

to the island of Maikalua, where a local steamer touched once a month. But poor Crusoe had no such contented mind. His is a tragic story, albeit considered so entertaining for schoolboys : and though his stay on the island taught him to find religion it did not teach him to find happiness, but whether at work or at leisure he was always looking with a restless and haggard stare at the rigid horizon, watching for a sail, enemy or friend, he knew not.

' I see numbers of goats. Melancholy reflections.' What a world of sombre and attentive ennui, thought Mr. Fortune, is summed up in those words ! The goats might supply him with suppers and raiment, but not with a cheerful thought. Their antics were wasted on him, he observed them without a smile, without sympathy, as unresponsive to natural history as the traduced Alexander Selkirk of Cowper's poem ; for the real Alexander was a much more genial character who sometimes danced and sang with his troop of pet animals. True, Robinson was fond of his dog, and kind to him, setting him on his right hand at meal-times even after he was grown ' very old and crazy.' He also gave decent burial to the two cats. But these were English animals, fellow-countrymen, assuring relics of the time when he had been knolled to church with other Christians : and it was for this he cherished them, clinging to them with a trivial and desperate affection.

No ! In spite of his adventurous disposition and his knowledge of the world, he was not really suited to life on an island, this man who is for all time the representative of island-dwellers. Of course, his island was very different from Fanua : larger, not so beautiful probably ; certainly not so convenient. And no doubt the presence of natives would have made a great difference to him. He was the sort of man who would soon marry. ' But to be honest with myself,' thought Mr. Fortune, ' though I came here to convert the islanders, except for my Friday I don't think I should miss their company if it were withdrawn. My happiness is of a rather selfish and dream-like kind and I take my life very much for granted. Why, I have not even walked round the island. That would seem strange to some, they would not believe in me. I should seem as absurd and idyllic as those other Robinsons, that Swiss family, who whenever they needed anything found it cast up on the shore or growing on a tree. I should be even more unlikely than Leila.'

And he began to ponder on how many years had gone by since he last thought of Leila. She came in a book belonging to his step-sister, and he had read it secretly and rather bashfully, because it was a book for girls. But he had been obliged to read on, for the subject of islands had always enthralled him. Leila was shipwrecked on a desert island with her papa, her nurse, a spaniel, and a needle. One day the needle was dropped by Leila and lost in the sand. Here was a sad to-do ! But the nurse, a very superior politic woman, bade the spaniel 'Go seek'; and presently he uttered a yelp and came running towards them with the needle sticking in his nose.

A very thin story ! Yet it might have happened for all that it was so fortunate. Things do sometimes fall out as we would have them, though perhaps not often, for it is always the happy coincidences which are hardest to credit. Man, however gullible and full of high ideals for his own concerns, is suspicious of good-fortune in general. If Robinson had enjoyed himself on the island

he would not have been received as somebody in real life.

' But I am in real life,' thought Mr. Fortune, adroitly jerking a limpet to assure
himself of being so, ' although I am so
happy in my lot. I am real too, as real as
Robinson. Some people might even say I
was more real than he, because my birth is
mentioned in the church register, and I used
to pay income-tax, whereas he was only
entered at Stationers' Hall. But I don't
agree with them. I may seem to have the
advantage of him now, but it is only tem-
porary. In twenty years' time, maybe less,
who will even remember my name ? '

From such reflections he would be diverted
by Lueli politely handing him a long
streamer of seaweed, dripping and glistening, and freshly exhaling its deep-sea smell—
a smell that excites in one strongly and
mysteriously the sense of life—or beckoning
to him with a brown hand that held a silver
fish. These advances meant that Lueli
thought it time for Mr. Fortune to bathe too,
and to take his swimming-lesson—a turning
of the tables which the convert considered
extremely amusing and satisfactory.

He was a very poor pupil. As a child he

had never done more than paddle about, and now he was too old to learn easily. He did not lack goodwill or perseverance, but he lacked faith. Faith which can remove mountains can also float. Mr. Fortune had not enough of it to do either. In the depths of his heart he mistrusted the sea, an ambiguous element. The real sea beyond the reef he never dreamed of venturing in, he could imagine how the long nonchalant rollers would pick him up and hurl him with their casual strength upon the rocks. Even in this sheltered pool he could gauge their force ; for though scarcely a ripple traversed the surface, to every leisurely surge that crashed on the reef the pool responded throughout its depth with a thrill, a tremor, an impulsion, and the streamers of seaweed turned inland one after another as though they were obeying a solemn dance music.

But for all his mistrust he enjoyed bathing, indeed the mistrust put a tang into his enjoyment. And with looks of derring-do he struck out into the middle of the pool, his teeth set, his eyes rolling, splashing horribly and snorting a good deal, labouring himself along with uncouth convulsions, while Lueli swam beside him or round him or under him

as easily as a fish and with no more commo-
tion, seeming like a fish to propel himself and
change his direction with an occasional
casual flip.

The further half of the pool, under the wall
of rock whence Lueli used to dive, was extremely deep. Whenever he had got so far
Mr. Fortune was afraid and not afraid. He
had a natural fear, but he had a reasonable
trust ; for he knew that while Lueli was by
he would never drown. It was sweet to him
to be thus relying upon his convert—that
was part of the pleasure of bathing. On
shore it was fit and proper that Lueli should
look up to him and learn from him ; but
every affectionate character, even though it
be naturally a dominant one, spending itself
by rights in instruction and solicitude, likes
sometimes to feel dependent. People, the
most strong-minded people, perfectly accustomed to life, being ill may discover this ;
and as they lie there, passive, tended, and a
little bewildered, may be stirred to the
depths of their being by finding themselves
wrapped once more in the security of being
a good child. Mr. Fortune bathing in the
pool did not go quite so far as this. His
dependence was not quite so emotional and

he was too busy keeping himself afloat to
analyse his feelings very carefully ; but he
liked to depend on Lueli, just as he liked
Lueli to depend on him.

Though so ready to learn swimming from
Lueli he was less favourably inclined to
another of his convert's desires : which was
to oil him. He would not for the world have
had Lueli guess it ; but at the first proposal
of these kind offices he was decidedly shocked.
Lueli oiled himself as a matter of course, and
so did everybody on the island. They also
oiled each other. Mr. Fortune had no objection. It was their way. But below all
concessions to broad-mindedness his views on
oiling were positive and unshakable. They
were inherent in the very marrow of his
backbone, which was a British one. Oiling,
and all that sort of thing, was effeminate,
unbecoming, and probably vicious. It was
also messy. And had Hector and Achilles,
Brutus and Alexander defiled before him, all
of them sleek and undeniably glistening as
cricket-bats, he would have been of the same
opinion still.

' No, thank you,' he said, firmly putting
aside the flask of scented coco-nut oil
(scented, too !). Or : ' Not just now, Lueli,

I am going for a walk. Exercise is the best thing after bathing.' Or again : ' Unfortunately oil has a very painful effect on my skin.'

But he knew all the time that sooner or later he would have to muffle up his prejudices and give in, for every day Lueli began to look, first more hopeful and then more hurt, and was perpetually (if figuratively) standing on his head in the attempt to produce some unguent which could not injure his friend's sensitive skin. So when he sprained his knee jumping off a rock he welcomed the pretext with feelings intricately compounded of relief and apostasy. For some weeks he confined the area of effeminacy to his left knee, and on one occasion he was base enough to lacerate the flesh in secret with a fish-hook in an attempt to justify the statement about his skin. But Lueli was so piteously full of compunction and so certain that if he climbed a yet higher tree or went in a canoe to another island he would be able to procure a balm entirely blameless, that Mr. Fortune was ashamed of the prank and counterfeited no more. Indeed he was beginning to enjoy what he assured himself was not oiling, nothing of the sort, but a purely medicinal process. And by the time he had finished with the sprain it struck him that something of the same kind might be good for his rheumatism. After all there was nothing but what was manly and might quiet him in Elliman's Embrocation—used extensively by many athletes and as far as he could remember by horse-doctors.

Mr. Fortune kept his rheumatism up and down his back, but inevitably a little of the embrocation slopped over his shoulders. By the end of six months he was stretching himself out for Lueli's ministrations as methodically as when in the old days at the corner of the Hornsey Parade he offered one foot and then the other to the boot-black. It did him a great deal of good, and improved his appearance tenfold, though that did not matter to him. Nothing could make him fat, but he began to look quite well-liking. The back of his hands grew smooth and suent, he ceased to have goose-flesh on his thighs, and one day, regarding himself more attentively than usual in the little shaving mirror, he discovered that somehow his expression had changed. How and why he would not stoop to examine into ; but Lueli

could have told him. For when he came
to the island his face was so parched and
wrinkled that it was like a mask of rough
earthenware, and his eyes, being the only
surface in it that looked alive, also looked
curiously vulnerable. But now his face had
come alive too, and instead of wrinkles had
rather agreeable creases that yielded and
deepened when he laughed. And his eyes
were no longer vulnerable, but just kind.

But if Mr. Fortune had altered during his
three years on the island, Lueli had altered
a great deal more. Not in character though—
he was still the same rather casual compen-
dium of virtues and graces; nor in behaviour;
for he still hung affectionately and admir-
ingly round Mr. Fortune with a dependence
which, for all its compliance and intimacy,
yet remained somehow gaily and coolly
aloof, so that the priest felt more and more
that what he was rearing up was in truth a
young plant, a vine or a morning glory,
which, while following all the contours of the
tree it clings to, draws from its own root alone
a secret and mysterious life in which the very
element of dependence is as secret and
mysterious as the rest.

In the beginnings of an intimacy one seems

to be finding out day by day more about another person's inner life and character. But after a certain stage has been reached not only does further exploration become impossible but things which one thought were discoveries become suddenly quite meaningless and irrelevant, and one finds that one really knows nothing about them, nothing at all. They sit beside one, they turn their heads and make some remark, and the turn of the head and the tone of the voice and even what they say seem all familiar and already recognised in one's heart : but there can be no knowing why they turned and spoke at that moment and not at another, nor why they said what they did and not something totally different. Though one might expect this realisation to be agonising, it is so much part of the natural course of things that many people do not notice it at all, and others, whilst acknowledging that something has happened, account for it perfectly to their own satisfaction by hypotheses which are entirely inapplicable.

Mr. Fortune, for instance, finding that he knew no more of Lueli than at the moment when he first beheld him kneeling on the grass, said to himself that he now knew him

so well that he had grown used to him. In
the same breath he was able to rejoice in a
confidence that no phase of Lueli's development could catch him napping ; and he
plumed himself on his acuteness in observing
that Lueli was growing older every day and
was now of an age to assert himself as a
young man.

For all that, Mr. Fortune could never
quite compass thinking of him as such.
Time in this pleasant island where the
seasons passed so lightly and where no one
ever showed the smallest sense of responsi-
bilty was like a long happy afternoon spent
under the acacia with the children. However, Lueli was grown up (or would be, the
moment he noticed the fact himself), and
something would have to be done about it.
Something, particularly—for in matters of
this sort it is best to go straight to the point—
must be done about providing him with
a wife.

A Christian wife. And of late he had
made several inspections of the village with
this end in view, keeping an open eye for all
the young women, scanning them as search-
ingly as Cœlebs, artfully devising the like
cheese-paring tests for them and pondering

which would be the most eligible for conversion and holy matrimony. There were plenty of charming possibles—by now he had quite got over his empirical aversion to them as bevies—though at first sight they seemed more eligible for holy matrimony than for conversion, being, one and all, smiling, wholesome, and inclined to giggle. But of course convertibility was the prime consideration. Perhaps by catching his hare and making a special effort? Mr. Fortune admitted that during this last year his labours as a missionary had been growing rather perfunctory.

Not that he loved his flock less. Rather he loved them more, and to his love was added (and here was the rub) a considerable amount of esteem. For seeing the extraordinarily good hand they made at the business of living to their own contentment —a business that the wise consider so extremely laborious and risky—and reflecting that for all their felicity they yet contrived to do nobody any harm, he felt some diffidence in his mission to teach them to do better.

And then he would pull himself up with a jerk and remember fiercely that they were

loose livers and worshipped idols. Moreover they had rejected the word of God, and
had made their rejection if anything worse
by making it with such flippancy and un-
concern. The seed he scattered had fallen
into a soil too rich and easy, so that the weeds
sprang up and choked it. Alas, all their
charming good qualities were but a crop of
fragrant and exotic groundsel, and their
innocence was like the pure whiteness and
ravishing classical contours of the blossom
of the common bindweed, which strangles
the corn and looks up from the crime with
its exquisite babyface.

Yet after all (he consoled himself by
thinking), the apparent reluctance of the
Fanuans to become Christians might all
be part of God's dealings. God proceeds
diversely in divers places, and where His
servants have prepared the ground for wheat
He may overrule them and set barley. In
some islands He may summon the souls with
a loud immediate thunderclap ; in others
He would go about it differently, knowing
the secrets of all hearts. God's time is the
best. And perhaps it was His intention in
Fanua to raise up a people from the marriage
of Lueli as He had prepared Himself a

people in the seed of Abraham and Sarah.
At this thought Mr. Fortune went off into
one of his dreams, and he grew cold with
emotion as he gazed into the future, seeing
in a vision Lueli's children and grand-
children and great-grandchildren, mild and
blessed, stretching away into the distance
like a field of ripened wheat which the wind
flows over and the sun shines on. They
would remember him, for their fathers would
have told them. But No (he thought), there
was no need for them to remember him.
For it is only the unsatisfied who want to be
remembered : old Simeon in the fullness of
his joy, beholding the light and the glory,
had no plea but to depart in peace.

Meanwhile, which girl ? Ori's tall
daughter, gentle Vaili, or the little plump
one who laughed so much that he could
never remember her name ? It occurred
to him that since it was Lueli's wife he was
choosing Lueli might well be consulted.

Lueli was out fishing. Mr. Fortune sat
till dusk by the spring, thinking out what he
would say and choosing his metaphors and
turns of speech with unusual pleasure and
care as though he were preparing a sermon.

The long shadows had merged into shadow

and the western sky was a meditative green
when Lueli returned. In one hand he held
a glistening net of fish and in the other a
bough of fruit, so that he looked like some
god of plenty, a brown slip of Demeter's who
had not got into the mythology.

Mr. Fortune admired the fish and admired
the fruit ; but inwardly he admired Lueli
more, this beautiful young man smelling of
the sea. He gave a little cough and began
his speech.

Marriage, he said, was a most excellent
thing. It was God's first institution, and in
the world's loveliest garden the flowers had
asked no better than to be twined into a
wreath for the bride. Men's stories com-
monly end with a marriage, but in God's
story the marriage comes at the beginning.
The ancient poets when they would cele-
brate the sun compared him to a bridegroom, the saints could find no tenderer
name for Christ than the spouse of the soul,
and in the vision of the last things John the
Evangelist saw the church descending out
of Heaven like a bride, so that God's
story which begins with a mortal marriage ends with a marriage too, but an
immortal one.

What did Lueli think ? Did he not agree that marriage was a good thing ?

Lueli nodded. His face wore an admiring and far-away expression, as though he were listening to the harmonium.

Marriage, Mr. Fortune continued, is a gracious act, a bestowal, and a token of man's gratitude to his Maker. When we are happy we needs must give ; Lueli himself was always giving, be it fruit or fish, a strand of seaweed or a flower. These gifts are transient and incomplete : the weed begins to lose its gloss from the moment it is taken out of the ocean ; the fish and the fruit (unless, of course, eaten) go bad ; the flower is broken from the stem, its petals will discolour and fold up in death ; but whoever begets children gives life itself, gives that from which all gifts are drawn.

The procreation of children is the first end for which marriage is ordained. But that was not all. There was also the love of man and woman and the pleasure they had in one another's company. When he was a young man, Mr. Fortune said, he had often wished for a wife to be merry with. Now he was too old to think much of such things, but none the less marriage did not seem to him less desirable, for now he understood as he did not and could not in his youth how sweet it would be to have the faithful company of one with whom he had shared his best days, if it were only, as a celebrated English Divine once expressed it in a sermon, that he might have some one to whom he could say : ' How our shadows lengthen as our sun goes down ! '

Mr. Fortune stopped. Lueli's silent consenting and his own thoughts had led him too far. He had not meant to introduce such serious considerations into a discourse on marriage, and the mournful sound of his own voice alone in the shadow of night suddenly revealed to him that he was sorrowful, although he had not thought he was.

' Tell me, Lueli, have you thought at all about whom you would prefer ? '

' Vaili is a nice girl and her father would give her a good dowry——'

Lueli pressed up the tip of his nose with the tip of his finger and spoke in a soft considering voice.

' Or there is Fuma, or Lepe who loves singing. But I think Vaili would suit you best, so you had better marry her.'

' I marry ! No, no, Lueli, you are mis-

taken, I was not talking of myself but of you.
It is your marriage I was thinking about.'

' Oh ! Were you ? '

' Wouldn't you like a wife, Lueli ? As
you were saying, Vaili is a nice girl. She is
gentle and fond of children, we could soon
teach her to become a Christian if we gave
our minds to it. I 'm sure you could be
very happy with Vaili.'

A decided shake of the head.

' Fuma, then.'

Another shake.

' Well, what about Lepe or Tialua ? '

Mr. Fortune proceeded to recite the names
of all the girls on the island, feeling not very
respectable as he did so, but going stead-
fastly on because he was in for it now, he
could not go back on his own sermon. But
he might as well have recited the Kings of
Israel and Judah or the Queens consort of
England from Matilda of Flanders down to
Adelaide of Saxe-Meiningen for all the effect
it had on Lueli, who sat beside him listening
decorously as though to a lesson and silently
waving away each one of Mr. Fortune's
nominees.

' But, Lueli, if you don't approve of any
of these, whom do you want ? '

A terrible possibility had flashed upon
him. Suppose, like the traditional young
man, Lueli had placed his affections on
some mature married woman ? What steps
should he take, indeed what steps could he
take ? He would not even have public
opinion on his side.

' I don't want any one. I am quite happy
as I am.'

' But, Lueli, you are young and vigorous.
This is not natural and I don't think it is at
all advisable. Why, St. Paul himself——'
And Mr. Fortune gave a short summary of
St. Paul's views on the marrying or burning
question, toning them down a little, for
privately he considered the saint's con-
clusions a trifle acrid. But there was no
shaking Lueli, who continued to asseverate
that he found chastity an easier matter than
St. Paul supposed, and in any case preferable
to the nuisance of taking a wife.

It seemed rather odd and improbable to
Mr. Fortune, but he let the matter drop and
did not speak of it again. Lueli would
change his tune all in good time no doubt.
Meanwhile things could go on as before, and
certainly nothing could be pleasanter. Of
course he was properly desirous to see the

beginnings of that Christian family, and he was much looking forward to becoming a godfather. He had already settled that since the proper consecrated kind of mugs were unprocurable, the first child should have the teapot and the second the sovereign he still kept for luck. After that he supposed he would have to sacrifice the magnifying-glass and the tuning-fork, and after that again— well, he still had time to think about it. Indeed, at present even the teapot seemed to be indefinitely postponed.

He was puzzled by Lueli, but he was not uneasy about him ; when he went off by himself he did not speculate as to what he was up to, nor ask strategic questions on his return. He trusted the boy and he also trusted himself. He did not think he could be deceived in Lueli.

And so things went kindly and easily on till the day when he was to find out his mistake.

It was very hot weather. Mr. Fortune had been suffering from a severe headache, and had spent the whole day lying down in the shade with wet cloths on his head. About sundown he decided to go for a short stroll, hoping that the dusk and the cool airs from the sea would refresh him. He called for Lueli to come too, but Lueli was nowhere about, so he set forth alone, crossing the dell and going down toward the sea. As he went he admired the brilliance of the after-glow, a marvellous rose-coloured bloom that seemed to hang on the air like a cloud of the finest metallic dust. Perhaps his eyes were weakened by headache and so more sensitive to light than usual ; but as he roamed up and down the shadowy strand, at each turn that brought him to face the west he mar-velled, thinking that in all his evenings at Fanua he had never beheld the sky so vibrating with colour nor so slow to fade— for sunsets in the tropics are fleeting things, but to-night there was a strange steadfastness in the west. He admired it so much that it was not possible for him to admire it for very long, and there was still light in the sky as he turned homeward.

Ordinarily he kept to the same routes as faithfully as though they had been ruled for him with red ink. But to-night, lost in thoughts of he knew not what, he strayed from his direction and found himself ap-proaching a little grove of coco-palms. They grew prettily together, laced with creepers and thickened with an undergrowth of ferns ; there was something about the innocence of their arrangement which reminded him of an English copse, and the resemblance was increased by a little path that turned and twisted its way in among them. But in an English copse even the slenderest path is wide enough for two lovers to walk it with their arms about each other, while this path was so narrow that it was clearly the path of one who visited the thicket alone.

A parrot flew off from a bough above his head, uttering a loud cry. Mr. Fortune roused himself from his dream. He was not in an English copse, looking for bluebells and being careful not to tread on a nightingale's nest, he was in a grove of coco-palms on the island of Fanua, an island in the midst of the Pacific Ocean like an island in a story-book. And he was looking for——? He was not looking for anything ; for in all his time at Fanua though he admired the flowers he had rarely picked any. It did not occur to him to do so. One picks only the flowers that one learned to pick as a child—cowslips and primroses and cuckoo-pint, and pale starwort that grows in the dusty summer hedge and fades before one can carry it home.

Lueli was always picking flowers. Perhaps he came here for them, perhaps he had been along this path but an hour ago? At any rate some flower-gatherer had; for lying at his feet Mr. Fortune observed a dark-coloured blossom like a stain. He stooped and picked it up. Yes, it was freshly gathered, it had not begun to wither yet, but it was moist with dew and felt cold and forsaken.

Presently Mr. Fortune came on a trail of lilac-flowered creeper caught up on a fern. He disentangled this and carried it along with him.

'Extravagant creature!' he said; for now he felt sure that he was on Lueli's track. 'I could make myself a bouquet out of what he spills and scatters.'

He still followed the path, wondering what next he would pick up. A little further on he perceived a whole garland lying on a patch of greensward. He was in the heart of the little wood, and here the path seemed to end.

'I declare that he's still child enough to be playing at houses. And this is the young man I've been trying to find a wife for!'

It looked exactly as though Lueli had been

playing at house. The ferns and bushes around were hung with trailing sprays of blossom which looped them into a pretence of being walls, and in the midst beside the garland was a platter arranged with fruits and leaves.

' What a child ! ' exclaimed the priest. ' Yet after all it may not be Lueli. Why should I be so sure that this is his fancy-work ? '

In an instant he was to be made quite sure. Something slim and dusky and motionless was reared up behind the platter of fruit. He looked closer. It was dreadfully familiar. He snatched it up and stared close into its face, a face he had seen before. And trampling on the garland he stood glaring at Lueli's idol, which looked back at him with flowers behind its ears.

It was quite obvious, quite certain. There was no chance of being mistaken, no hope of doubt. For all these years Lueli had been playing a double game, betraying him, feigning to be a Christian, and in secret, in the reality of secretness, worshipping an idol.

' It is my fault,' said the priest, speaking aloud because of his desperate loneliness.

'Not his at all, nor yours either,' and he gave the idol a sort of compassionate shake.

'I have deluded myself wilfully, I have built my house on the sand. . . .'

'I have forgotten the fear of God,' he went on. 'All this time I have gone on pretending that religion is a pleasant, is a gentle thing, a game for good children.'

'But it is an agony!' he suddenly shouted out.

There was no echo. The sultry twilight was closing in on him like a dark fleece. He could scarcely see the idol now, but in his mind's eye he could see it, a face coldly and politely attentive, and the narrow polished shoulders over which a doll's necklace slipped and sidled as it shook with his trembling hands.

'It is torments, wounds, mutilation, and death. It is exile and weariness. It is strife—an endless strife—it is bewilderment and fear and trembling. It is despair.'

Turning abruptly he left the thicket by the path which had led him in, and stumbling in the dark and feeling his body heavy and cold in the hot night he made his way back to the hut.

It was all dark; but that was no reason

why Lueli should not be within, for he had been so often warned to handle the lamp carefully that he was a coward about it and never touched it if he could avoid doing so.

Mr. Fortune threw down the idol and lit the lamp from his tinder-box. Then he looked round. Lueli was curled up on his mat. He had been asleep, and now he opened his eyes and looked drowsily at his friend. Mr. Fortune said nothing. He stood in the centre of the hut under the hanging lamp and waited for Lueli to notice the idol.

Lueli parted his lips. He was just about to speak when he saw what lay on the ground. He raised his eyes to Mr. Fortune's countenance, for a moment he put on a confused smile, then with an ill-feigned yawn he turned over and pretended to have fallen asleep again.

' Deceit,' said Mr. Fortune, as though he were reading from a note-book.

A faint grunt answered him.

' Lueli, my poor Lueli, this is useless. You can't get out of it like this. Get up and tell me what it is that I have found.'

Lueli sat up. The pupils of his eyes were still distended by sleep and this gave him a frightened look ; but his demeanour was perfectly calm.

'That ? '

He shook his head as if to say that he really couldn't tell what it was.

'Look again.'

Mr. Fortune spoke curtly, but it was from pure sorrow.

'It is an idol.'

'Yes, and it is your idol.'

Lueli gave a sigh of distress. Mr. Fortune knew exactly how much that was worth. Lueli hated any unpleasantness.

'You don't ask me how I came by it. I found it in a thicket near the beach, the lonely one. And there were flowers round it, and offerings of fruit, and look, there are flowers stuck behind its ears.'

'So there are.'

'Is this your doing ? Why do I ask you, for I know it is. Lueli, you mustn't lie to me. I implore you not to lie. Is this your doing, have you been worshipping this object ? '

'I picked the flowers.'

Mr. Fortune groaned. Then he sat down like one who foresees a long and weariful business before him. Lueli edged himself a little nearer. He had rumpled up his brow

into a grimace of condolence, he looked like
a beautiful and sympathetic marmoset.

He said in a voice at once tender and sly:

'But why are you unhappy? I have
done nothing, it is only my idol, and I just
happened to pick it a few flowers. That
is all.'

'Listen. I will tell you why I am unhappy. When I came to Fanua I came to
teach you not to worship idols but to worship
God. I came to teach you all, but the
others would have none of me. You were
my only convert, you received my teaching,
I thought you loved it, and I trusted you.
Now I have found out my mistake. If you
worship your idol still I am to blame. It is
my fault. If I had done my duty by you
you would have known better. But I have
not shown you the true God, so you have
kept to the old one, the false one, a wooden
thing, a worship so false that you can treat
him like a toy. As I came back to-night I
was tempted with the thought that perhaps
after all your fault was only childishness.
And for a moment (to spare myself and you)
I had half a mind to pretend to God that
your idol was only a doll. But we will have
none of that.'

Now he spoke sternly, and at the last words he beat one fist against the other. Lueli started.

' I blame myself, I say, not you. I should have been on my guard. When I saw that thing two years ago I should have acted then. But I shut my eyes (I am most horribly to blame), and now, see what has come of it. You are in fault too, for you have been deceiving me. But I know you are rather cowardly and very affectionate ; your deceitfulness after all is not so surprising.'

He could have gone on talking like this for some time and finding it soothing, but he knew by experience that Lueli would find it soothing too. He raised his eyes from his heavily folded hands and looked at the boy. Sure enough, there was the familiar expression, the lulled face of one who listens to a powerful spell.

He stopped short, nerved himself to deliver the blow, and said in a slow, dull voice :

' You must destroy your idol. You had better burn it.'

With a vehement gesture of refusal Lueli sprang to his feet.

' Burn it,' repeated the priest.

Such a wild and affronted antagonism defied him from the tautened brown body and the unswerving, unbeholding gaze that for a moment the priest was appalled. But his looks gave back defiance for defiance. They bore the other's down, and averting his eyes Lueli gave a sudden shrug and made as though to walk out of the hut.

Mr. Fortune was between him and the door. He jumped up and barred the line of retreat. Lueli wavered. Then he went back to his corner and sat down without a word. Mr. Fortune half-expected him to weep, but he did nothing so obliging.

For a good hour Mr. Fortune talked on, commanding, reasoning, expostulating, explaining, persuading, threatening. Lueli never answered him, never even looked at him. He sat with downcast eyes in utter stubbornness and immobility.

The night was sultry and absolutely still. Mr. Fortune dripped with sweat, he felt as though he were heaving enormous boulders into a bottomless pit. He continued to heave his words into silence, a silence only broken by the hissing of the lamp, or the creak of his chair as he changed from one uneasy position to another, but the pauses grew longer between each sentence. He was weary, and at his wits' end. But he could see nothing for it but to go on talking. And now he became so oppressed by the silence into which he spoke that he could foresee a moment when he would have to go on talking because he would be afraid to hold his tongue.

A frightful imagination took possession of him : that Lueli was become like his idol, a handsome impassive thing of brown wood, that had ears and heard not, that had no life in its heart. Would nothing move him ? He would have been thankful for a look of hate, for a curse or an insult. But with the same show of inanimate obstinacy Lueli continued to bend his look upon the ground, a figure too austere to be sullen, too much withdrawn into itself to be defiant.

Mr. Fortune heard himself say at the top of his voice : ' Lueli ! Don't you hear me ? '

It seemed that his outcry had broken the spell. Lueli suddenly looked up and began to listen, to listen with such strained, absorbed, animal attention that Mr. Fortune found himself listening too. There was a sound : a sound like a violent gust of wind strangely sweeping through the motionless night. It came rapidly, it came near, brushing its way through the tree-tops. Like an actual angry presence the wind came vehemently into the hut and, as though an invisible hand had touched it, Mr. Fortune saw the hanging lamp begin to sway. It swayed faster and faster, widening its sweep at every oscillation ; and while he stared at it in a stupor of amazement he felt the earth give a violent twitch under his feet as though it were hitting up at him, and he was thrown to the ground. There was a noise of rending and bellowing, the lamp gave a last frantic leap, again he felt the ground buffet him like the horns of a bull, and then with a crash and a spurt of fire the roof of the hut caved in.

At the same moment he felt something large and heavy topple across his body.

He could not move and he could not think. He saw flames rising up around him and heard the crackle of the dried thatch. Again the ground began to quiver and writhe beneath him, and suddenly he knew what was happening—an earthquake !

The bulk that lay on top of him was the harmonium. He was pinned beneath it— presently the flames would reach him and he would be burnt to death.

He felt no kind of fear or emotion, only a calm certainty as to what was happening and with it a curious detached satisfaction at being able to understand it all so well. The flames would enclose him and he would be burnt to death, unless the ground opened first and swallowed him up. Then he remembered Lueli. What of him? He struggled again, but he could not get out from under the harmonium. The struggle reminded him that he was a human being, not only an intelligence but a creature defencelessly sentient that must perish by fire. Fear came on him, and self-pity, and with it a sort of pique ; for he said to himself : ' I know now he never cared for me. He has made off and left me to burn, just what I should expect.' And at the same moment he heard himself cry out : ' Save yourself, Lueli ! Be quick, child ! Never mind me, I am all right.' And then, seeing Lueli bending over him, he said in a voice of command : ' Lueli, I tell you to save yourself. Get out of this while there 's time.'

He saw Lueli in the light of the flames, he saw him put his shoulder against the harmonium and begin to heave it up ; he saw the muscles leap out along the thrusting body—all with a sort of anger and impatience because his friend would not attend to what he was saying. Even when the harmonium was jolted backward and he was freed he lay where he had fallen, half-stunned, with no definite thought except to compel Lueli to obey him and get away before the next tremor sent the whole hut crashing down on them.

He felt Lueli put his arms round his shoulders, shaking him and hauling him on to his feet, and he noticed with surprise how stern the boy looked, not frightened, but extraordinarily stern, like a stranger, like an angel. The earth began to quake again, another sheaf of thatch slid from the roof and the flames leaped up to seize upon it. Mr. Fortune suddenly came out of his stupor. Stumbling and losing his footing on the wavering floor he caught hold of Lueli's arm and together they ran out of the hut.

Three times in crossing the dell they were thrown to the earth. There was something horribly comic in this inability to stand upright. It was as though they were being tossed in a blanket. They did not speak to each other ; all thought of speech was forbidden by the appalling novelty of the uproar that was going on, rumblings and bellowings underground, trees beating against each other or crashing to the earth, the cries of terror-struck creatures. Lueli dragged him on, hastening toward the mountain. There was a little path that led up by the ravine, difficult to mount at any time and more difficult still in an earthquake.

' Why do you go this way ? ' Mr. Fortune asked, when the tremor had subsided enough for him to be able to remember how to speak. Lueli turned on him a face of terror.

' The sea,' he said. ' The sea.'

Mr. Fortune had forgotten the sea. Now he remembered what he had read in books of adventure as a boy : how after an earthquake comes a tidal wave, a wall of water frantically hurling itself upon the land. And not daring to look behind him he followed Lueli up the steep path as though the sea were at his heels.

At last they came out upon a little grassy platform overlooking the ravine. They were only just in time, for the earthquake began again. They sat side by side, holding on to one another. Mr. Fortune discovered that it was a brilliant and impassive moonlight night. He looked toward the ocean. It seemed strangely calm, incredibly vast, more solid than the tormented earth. A glittering path of silver across it reflected the moon.

They were close to the cataract. To-night, instead of the usual steady roar of falling water, the noise was coming in curious gouts of sound, now loud, now almost nothing. He turned his eyes and saw the slender column of falling water all distorted, and flapping like a piece of muslin in a draught. For some reason this sight was overwhelmingly piteous and a sort of throe hollowed him as if he were going to cry.

At every shock thousands of birds flew up from the tossing tree-tops. In wild excite-ment they circled overhead, flying in droves, sweeping past with a whirr of innumerable wings, soaring higher and higher, then suddenly diving aslant, shot from the wake of their own vortex. Their continual angry clamour, passionate and derisive, swayed above the uproar of trampling earth and clashing forest. One bird came volleying so close to Mr. Fortune that he saw its beak flash in the moonlight and put up his hand to shield his face. As it passed it screamed in his ear like a railway whistle. He thought: ' I should like to scream like that.'

Although he and Lueli sat holding on to

each other, Mr. Fortune had no sense of companionship. In this appalling hour there did not seem to be any one alive save himself. He was the Last Man, alone in an universe which had betrayed him, abandoned on the face of an earth which had failed under his feet. He was isolated even from himself. There was no Mr. Fortune now, a missionary who had been a bank-clerk, an Englishman and a member of the Church of England. Such a one would have been behaving quite differently. At the best he might have been behaving much better, he might have been in the village keeping troth with his fellow-men ; at the least he would have been trembling for his own skin and calling on God. But this man sat on the reeling mountain side with but one sensation : a cold-hearted excitement, a ruthless attentive craving that at the height of horror would welcome another turn of the screw, another jab of the spur, another record broken.

The shocks were now coming so continuously that it was scarcely possible to say when one followed another ; but he went on keeping count and comparing them, and if they seemed to be slackening off he was disappointed. He sat with his eyes shut, for so he could both feel and hear more unmitigatedly. At intervals he looked out seaward for the coming of the tidal wave. But the sea was always calm, as coldly calm as himself and a great deal more solid. ' Yet it must come,' he told himself. ' It is certain to come.' And after a terrific shock, accompanied by sounds of rending and shattering as though the whole island were splitting asunder, he thought with certainty : ' It will come now,' and opened his eyes once more.

Something had happened. There was a difference in the air, in the colour of the night. Had dawn come already? His faculties were so cramped with attention that he could scarcely receive a new sensation, still less analyse it. Yet he felt that there was something he must account for, some discrepancy between this light and the light of dawn. The sun rose—yes, the sun rose in the east, over the sea : but this light seemed to come from behind him. He turned and saw the sky lit up with the light of fire.

' The mountain is on fire ! ' he cried out. And at the sound of his own words he suddenly understood what had happened. The mountain was on fire. Its ancient fires had come back to it, Fanua was once more an active volcano.

Below the bed of the cold and heavy sea, below the foundations of the great deep, into an unimaginable hell of energy and black burning those fires had withdrawn. They had rejoined the imprisoned original frenzy that lies in the heart of the earth, working and wallowing in unknown tides. And once more the fiery spring had mounted, revolting against the encompassing pressure, fumbling in darkness, melting its way, flooding along its former channels until now it flared on the crest of the island, brightening and brightening upon the sky, a glow of such intense and vivid rose-colour that by contrast the moonlight turned to an icily-piercing blue. Cloud upon cloud of smoke rolled upwards, and at every fresh surge of fire the vault of heaven appeared to grow more vast and haughty, and the stars seemed recoiling into space. The mountain shouted and bellowed as though it were triumphing because its fires had come back to it.

Mr. Fortune leapt to his feet. He waved his arms, he stood on tiptoe in order to see better. Though the next moment might engulf him he was going to make the most of

this. But there was no need to be so pro-
vident, so economical. This bonfire had
been preparing for decades, it would not
burn out in a minute or two. Realising this,
he sat down again and relinquished himself
to an entire and passive contemplation,
almost lulled by the inexhaustible procession
of fire and smoke, warming his mind at the
lonely terrific beauty of a mountain burning
by night amid an ocean.

Clouds began to gather at daybreak.
Only a pallor showed where the sun groped
upwards among them, and the sea, which
but a few hours ago had looked so lustrous,
and solid like a floor of onyx, was now pale
and weltering.

The earthquake seemed to be over ; sometimes the ground gave a sort of a twitch and
a tremble like an animal that dreams a bad
dream ; but this happened at longer and
longer intervals and each disturbance was
fainter than the last. Except for the plume
of foul smoke that issued from the crater and
sagged over the mountain side as it was
checked by the morning airs there was
nothing to distinguish this daybreak from
any other, unless, thought Mr. Fortune, that
it was a peculiarly dreary one.

He was chilled with watching, and oppressed with the indigestion common to those who have sat up all night. He was also bruised with so much falling about, and his ribs ached from being crushed under the harmonium. But his excitement, which in spite of all the adventures of the last twelve hours was still a deferred excitement, unsatisfied and defrauded of its prey, wouldn't let him settle down into a reasonable fatigue, but still kept his muscles strung up and his vision strained.

It seemed an age since he had last thought of Lueli. He looked at him now as though from a long way off, and rather crossly, and it seemed as though his vague irritation were in a way to be justified. For Lueli lay as though asleep.

That Lueli should sleep while he waked was enough. It showed that he was inconsiderate, incapable of true sympathy, an inferior being who hadn't got indigestion. Mr. Fortune heaved a loud short sigh. Lueli didn't stir. No doubt of it. He was asleep. He lay so that Mr. Fortune could only see the curve of his cheek and half his mouth, which bore the sad resigned expression of those who slumber. But bending a

little over him to make sure, Mr. Fortune
discovered that the boy's eyes were open
and fixed mournfully upon the empty and
unquiet sea. There was something so de-
vastated about that blank and unmoving
gaze that the priest was awed. Why did
Lueli look so old, so set and austere ? The
face so well known seemed that of a stranger ;
and suddenly he recalled Lueli bending
over him in the burning hut as he lay helpless under the harmonium, and remembered
that then his face had worn the same look,
grave and stern.

Lueli had saved his life at the risk of his
own, he had shown that greatest love which
makes a man ready to lay down his life for
his friend. And now the rescued one sat
coldly beside the rescuer, eyeing his unknown
sorrow, and but a moment ago seeking some
pretext for scorning and disliking him.

' What a hateful creature I am !' thought
Mr. Fortune, ' and how this earthquake has
shown me up ! But Lueli has behaved well
throughout, he saved my life, he kept his
head, he didn't want to cheer and behave
like a tripper when the mountain exploded.'
And in his thoughts he begged Lueli's
pardon.

Still Lueli lay beside him, staring out to sea with the same mournful look. His silence was like a reproach to Mr. Fortune. It seemed to say : ' You have slighted me unjustly and now I must forget you.' Mr. Fortune waited patiently, he had a confused idea that his patience now must repair his former impatience. But at length his love could endure no longer, and he laid his hand gently on Lueli's arm. There was no response. Lueli didn't even turn his eyes.

' He is tired out,' thought the priest. ' That is why he looks so miserable.' He said aloud : ' Wake up, Lueli, you will make yourself ill if you lie there any longer so still on the cold ground. Wake up. Rouse yourself. It is all over now.' And he gave him an encouraging slap on the shoulder.

At last Lueli sighed and stretched himself and turned and met Mr. Fortune's anxious gaze.

' I think the earthquake is over,' he remarked in an everyday voice.

' Just what I said a minute ago,' thought Mr. Fortune. ' But he doesn't know I said it. What can he have been thinking of that he didn't hear me ? '

He still felt slightly worried about the boy.

' We had better walk about a little,' he said. ' Ow ! I 've got cramp.'

Taking Lueli's arm he staggered down the little rocky path. The morning was cold and now it began to rain. The rain was dirty rain, full of smuts and fine grit from the volcano. It might have been raining in London or Manchester.

Exercise soon restored Mr. Fortune to an ordinary frame of mind. He looked with interested horror at the wood they passed through. Many trees were uprooted or hung tottering with their roots half out of the ground, the shrubs and grass were crushed and trampled, boughs and torn creepers were scattered everywhere. It was as though some savage beast had run amuck through the glades, tearing and havocking and rooting up the ground with its horns. Lueli picked up a dead parrot, and once they skirted by a swarm of angry bees. Their hive had been broken in the fall of its tree, the honeycomb was scattered on the grass, and the affronted insects were buzzing hither and thither, angrier than ever because now the rain was making its way through the dishevelled green roof.

' But it will soon quench them,' thought

Mr. Fortune. ' And if some bees and some parrots are the only deaths by this earth-quake we shall be well out of it.'

He was uneasy about the villagers, all the more so because he felt that he had run away from them in their hour of peril. Also he wanted to talk to some one about the stream of lava which he knew would soon flow down from the crater. ' Provided it only flows to the south ! ' he thought. He questioned Lueli but could learn nothing ; Lueli had never been in an earthquake before, he had heard the old men of the island talking about them but the last earthquake had happened long before his day.

On nearing the village Mr. Fortune heard a great hubbub, but it was impossible to discover from the noise of every one talking at once whether they were lamenting or merely excited ; all he could conclude was that at any rate they were not all dead.

When he appeared, with Lueli following sedately behind, a crowd of gesticulating islanders rushed forward, all waving their arms and shouting. The thought leapt up in his mind : ' Suppose they think that *I* am responsible for this earthquake ? Perhaps they will kill me to appease the mountain ! '

He had never felt less in the mood for martyrdom. The last twelve hours had given him more than enough to cope with. Yet even if the fervour of his faith were lacking, he could make a shift to die decently: and he stiffened himself and went forward. But Lueli? Suppose they wanted to martyr him too? No! That he would not allow. While there was a kick left in him he would see to that. He glanced back as though to reassure him, but as he caught sight of him he remembered that Lueli was not a Christian, nor ever had been one. What a sell if they should sacrifice him before there was time to explain! Well, this made it even more urgent a matter to defend him: martyrdom was one thing, miscarriage of justice quite another.

But Mr. Fortune need not have been agitated. The islanders had no intention but to welcome him and Lueli, and to rejoice round them over their safety, which they did with the pleasanter excitement and conviction, since naturally in the emotions of the night they had not given them a thought till now.

Half-smothered and quite deafened, Mr. Fortune pushed through the throng, saying:

' Where is Ori ? ' For having lived so long
on the island he had fallen into the proper
respect for a chief, and depended on Ori
rather more than he would have liked to
admit. ' He is almost like another European '—so the priest explained to himself.
At this juncture Ori was behaving very
much like an European, for he was partaking
of one of those emergency breakfasts, sketchy
in form but extremely solid and comprehensive in content, with which the white
races consummate and, as it were, justify any
fly-by-night catastrophe. Seeing Mr. Fortune he politely invited him to sit down and
take a share. ' But the flow of lava ? '
inquired Mr. Fortune, wiping his mouth.
' Do you think it will come this way ? ' Ori
took another handful of stirabout. ' There
are no signs of it so far, and if it comes this
way it will not come here yet.'

' But do you think it will come this way ? '

' My god says, No.'

When breakfast was finished Ori got up
and went off with the other men of conse-
quence to make an inquisition into the
damage done by the pigs. They had come
bolting down from the woods and wrought
even more serious havoc than the earth-

quake, which had only shaken down a house
or two, whereas the pigs had trespassed into
every enclosure and eaten all the provisions.
Mr. Fortune felt a little slighted that he was
not invited to go too. Apparently Ori did
not quite regard him as another Fanuan.
' Oh well,' he said, ' perhaps they meant it
politely, seeing that I had not finished
my breakfast.' But though he felt as
if he were hungry he had no real appetite,
and rising he prepared to walk back to his
hut.

It was as though the earthquake had
literally shaken his wits. All his recollec-
tions were dislodged and tumbled together ;
he knew they were there somewhere, but he
could not find them—just as he had mislaid
the discovery of overnight until, turning to
view Lueli as a possible martyr, he beheld
and recognised him as the idolater he was
and always had been. Now he was walking
to the hut in the same kind of oblivion. He
must have remembered the lamp tossing its
flame up to the roof, the burning sheaves of
thatch falling down around him, for he had
a very clear vision of Lueli's face bending
over him, so violently modelled by the flames
that it had looked like the face, sad and

powerful, of a stranger, of an angel. But his thoughts went no further ; and even when the smell of charred wood came sadly to his nostrils through the falling rain he did not put two and two together.

'I wonder if those pigs have messed up my place too,' he said. A sigh out of the air answered him. He had not noticed till then that Lueli was following.

'Poor Lueli, you must be so tired !' There was no answer and still the boy lagged behind. He must be tired indeed. Mr. Fortune stopped. He was about to speak once more, bidding Lueli to lean on him and take heart, when suddenly the boy shot past him, running desperately, and whispering to himself as he ran as though he were imploring his own mind.

Mr. Fortune hastened after him. Would all this strangeness, this bewilderment, this nightmare of familiar living confounded and turned backward never come to an end ? He hastened on into the smell of burning, and pulling aside the drooping fronds of a banana tree which, uprooted, had fallen and lay across the pathway like a screen, he beheld the ruins of the hut.

One wall was still standing, a few pale

flames licking wistfully over it. The rest was charred logs and hummocks of grey ash sizzling under the rain—for now it was raining more and more heavily. Looking round on the devastation he began to recognise the remains of his belongings. Those shreds of tinder were his clothes. That scrap of shrivelled leather, that wasting impalpable bulk of feathery print, was his Bible ; there lay the medicine chest and there the sewing-machine ; and this, this intricate ruin of molten metal tubes, charred rubber, and dislocated machinery, was the harmonium, its scorched ivory keys strewed round about it like teeth fallen from a monstrous head.

Lueli was there, but he seemed to have no thought for the unfortunate priest amid the ruins of his home. Wading among the hot ashes, crouching close to the wreckage, turning over this and that with rapid and trembling hands, Lueli was searching with desperate anxiety for—Mr. Fortune knew not what. At length he gave a bitter cry and cast himself down upon the ground.

Instantly Mr. Fortune was kneeling beside him, patting his shoulder, trying to lift the averted head.

'What is it, Lueli? What is it, my dear, dear friend?'

Lueli sat up and turned on him a face discoloured and petrified into an expression of such misery that he could hardly endure to look at it.

'What is it? Are you hurt? Are you ill?'
The expression never changed.

'Are you frightened, Lueli? Has it upset you to find our home burnt to the ground? But never mind! We will soon have another, it is nothing to grieve for.'

He would have said that Lueli did not hear him, so unmoving he sat, so utterly aloof, but that at these last words a very slight smile of scorn quivered on the dry lips.

Then Mr. Fortune remembered. He hung his head; and when he spoke again it was with the grave voice in which we address the bereaved.

'Is it your god you were looking for? Is he gone?'

Lueli did not answer. But it was clear that he had both heard and understood, for he fixed his eyes on the priest's face with the look of an animal which knows itself at man's mercy but does not know what man intends to do to it.

' My poor Lueli ! Is that it ? . . . Is it
so dreadful ? Yes, I know it must be, I
know, I know. I would do anything to
comfort you, but I cannot think how, I can
only tell you how I pity you with my whole
heart. I do, indeed I do. Believe me,
though I told you to burn your god, yet at
this moment, if it were possible for me, I
think I would even give it to you again.'

He spoke very slowly, scarcely daring to
lift his gaze to the sorrow which sat beside
him, not answering, not crying out, meek
with the meekness of despair. And still
Lueli listened, and still looked, with his
expression wavering between timidity and
antagonism.

' Lueli, I spoke very harshly to you last
night, not like a Christian, not as one sad
human being should speak to another. In
blaspheming against your god I blasphemed
against my own. And now I can't comfort
you. I don't deserve to. I can only sit
beside you and be sorry.'

Lueli never answered, and Mr. Fortune
acted his last words, sitting mournfully beside him in the rain. After an hour or so
Lueli began to topple forward, then suddenly he lay down and fell asleep.

Now Mr. Fortune had time to think, and though he was dog-tired think he must. For after a while Lueli would wake again, and then the missionary must have some settled reasonable comfort for him, some plan of consolation. On the face of it nothing could be clearer. He should say something of this sort : ' Your god, Lueli, was only made of wood, perishable and subject to accidents, like man who is made of flesh. He is now burnt, and his ashes are lost among the other ashes. Now will you not see that my God is a better God than yours, and turn to Him ? For my God is from everlasting, even though the earth shake He cannot be moved.'

Yes, that was the sort of thing to say, but he felt a deep reluctance to saying it. It seemed ungentlemanly to have such a superior invulnerable God, part of that European conspiracy which opposes gun-boats to canoes and rifles to bows and arrows, which showers death from the mountains upon Indian villages, which rounds up the negro into an empire and tricks him of his patrimony.

Mr. Fortune remembered the Man of Sorrows. Would Lueli accept in the place of his wooden god a God that had once been made flesh ? In the old days Lueli had enjoyed hearing about Jesus, though Mr. Fortune had always suspected him of preferring Joshua. Many, very many, must have taken Jesus to their hearts out of pity, following the example of the woman who washed His feet, although to her they were most likely but the feet of a wayfaring man. But it was rare to find a Polynesian accepting Him for these mortal motives, they themselves were not sorrowful enough. Probably, despite the loss of his god, Lueli would still prefer the more robust and stirring character of Joshua.

The trumpet that shall awaken the dead with the sanction of the resurrection is louder than all the rams' horns that blew down Jericho. As an honest priest it was Mr. Fortune's duty to preach not only Christ crucified but also Christ arisen to comfort His followers awhile with neighbourly humanity ere He ascended to His Father. If this were all, it might suit Lueli very well : but in a twinkling it would lead him on to the Trinity, a mysterious sign revolving in the heavens from everlasting, a triangle that somehow is also a sphere. And so he was back again where he started from, embarrassed with a God so superior to poor Lueli's that to insist upon Him now would be heartless boasting, would be exploiting an unfair advantage, wouldn't be cricket.

' If I were a proper missionary,' he burst out in a cross voice. And then with a wry grin he added : ' It doesn't look as though I were any sort of missionary. Lord, what a mess I 've made of it ! '

He had indeed. The mess amid which he sat was nothing to it. Disconsolately he looked at his watch. It had stopped. In the stress of overnight he had forgotten to wind it up, and now it recorded the epoch at which his last link with European civilisation had been snapped—eight hours thirty-five minutes. It could not be much later than that now. But a miss is as good as a mile, and for the rest of his sojourn on the island, for the rest of his life maybe, he would not know what o'clock it was. This circumstance, not serious in itself and not to be compared with the loss of the medicine chest or his books, upset him horribly. He felt frightened, he felt as small and as desperate as a child lost. ' I must set it as best I can,' he thought. ' After all, time is a convention, just like anything else. My watch will measure out my days and remind me to be up and doing just as well though it be a little askew. And no doubt I shall die at my appointed hour, however erroneously I reckon to it.'

But what time was it? The sky was overcast, he could not guess by the sun and he could not guess by his own time-feeling either, for his body had lost touch with ordinary life. He sat debating between nine-seventeen, five past ten, ten-forty-three, eleven-twenty—indecisive times which all seemed reasonably probable—and noon exactly, which was bracing and decisive, a good moment to begin a new era—but too good to be true. At last he settled on ten-twenty-five ; but even so he still delayed, for he felt a superstitious reluctance to move the hands and so to destroy the last authentic witness his watch could bear him. Five minutes, he judged, had been spent in this weak-minded dallying : so resolutely he set the hands to ten-thirty and wound the poor machine up. It began to tick, innocently, obediently. It had set out on its fraudulent career.

It was a good watch, painstaking and punctual, its voice was confident, it had an honest face ; but henceforth its master had lost his trust in it, and though he wore it (like a wife) at bed and at board and wound it up regularly and hung it on a tree when he went bathing, yet he never could feel it was his true wife (watch, I mean) again.

Still Lueli slept.

' I make all this fuss,' thought Mr. Fortune, ' I even feel helpless and abandoned, because I have lost my reckoning of time. How much worse to lose one's god ! '

Thus, the watch diversion over and done with, and the new time being ten-thirty-one, he was back on the old problem. What could he do for poor Lueli who had lost his god ? ' And it was for me that he lost it,' he thought, with a poignancy of feeling that was almost irritation. ' He might have picked up his god and run out of the hut with it, but he would not leave me under the harmonium.' It was heroic, desperately heroic. . . . Yet there might have been time to save both ? A god that could be picked up in one hand. Had Lueli in the flurry of the moment forgotten that the idol lay on the floor of the hut ? ' But No, one would not forget one's god,' thought he, ' even in an earthquake.'

Now he could understand why Lueli had seemed so cold in the early morning, so aloof and unlike his usual self. When he had lain staring out to sea with that strange expression he had been tasting what it feels like to be without a god. And when they approached the hut that was why he had lagged behind until the last explosion of hope had sent him running to seek his god among the wood-ashes. Now he was asleep. But he would not sleep much longer. Already he had stirred once or twice, and sighed, as those do who must soon awaken. And still Mr. Fortune had not settled how to deal with him when he awoke. Would the Man of Sorrows fit his sorrowful case, He who had once cried out, *Eloi, Eloi, lama sabachthani*? Or would it be better to try Jehovah, a tribal character whose voice was in the clouds, whose arrows stuck very fast? The worst of it was that Lueli knew all about them already. For three years he had been living on the terms of the greatest intimacy with them, he was even at home with the Trinity. And so all that Mr. Fortune could tell him now would be but a twice-told tale ; and that was not likely to be of much effect, for Polynesians are fickle, they

tire as easily as children and must be bribed
with novelties.

Mr. Fortune grew increasingly despond-
ent. He was even growing bored, and more
and more quickly he turned over in his mind
the various expedients of Godhead which
might appeal to Lueli, like a woman tossing
over a piece-bag in search of something she
cannot find. The blue print, the grey
merino, the long and ever more tangled
trail of metal lace, a scrap of corduroy : none
of these is what she looks for, and what she
looks for is not there.

' I can do nothing,' he cried out ; and
then an inner voice finishing the quotation
for him added, ' without Thee.'

Of course he could do nothing without
God. Why had he not thought of that
before ? Why, instead of vain thinking,
hadn't he prayed ?

He looked about him. He was alone in a
mesh of rain. For leagues around the rain
was falling, falling upon the quenched ashes
of his homestead where were mingled and
quenched too the ashes of Lueli's god, falling
upon the motionless forest, falling upon the
moving ocean, on that vast watery and in-
divisible web of tides and currents, falling

everywhere with an equal and unstaying pressure. Only upon the newly open mouth of the pit was the rain not falling, for there the flames rushed up and caught and consumed it.

There had been an earthquake and now it was raining. Both events were equally natural, equally accountable for, equally inevitable. There was nowhere any room for chance ; no happening from the greatest to the least could be altered or provoked or turned aside. And why should he specify into greatest or least ? In causation there is no great or small. He himself was as great as the mountain, as little as the least of the ashes of Lueli's god.

Still he looked about him. But he was not looking for anything now, nor did he need to raise his eyes to heaven or close them before any presence unseen. The God who had walked with him upon the island was gone. He had ascended in the flames that had burst roaring and devouring from the mountain-top, and hiding His departure in clouds of smoke He had gone up and was lost in space.

Mr. Fortune no longer believed in a God. It had all happened quite quietly, just like that.   Once he put out his hand as though to arrest something that was floating away out of reach, but in a moment it dropped again. And there it was before him, resting upon his knees, the hand of a man who didn't any longer believe in a God, with fingers idly patting out a slow and flagging rhythm, tick-tock, like a time-piece that is running down. The real time-piece went on nimbly enough, it was now (he noticed) five minutes to eleven of the new era.   If his diary had not been burnt he could have mentioned in it with impressive accuracy : ' At 10.54 A.M. (N.T.) I ceased to believe in God.'   This quaint fancy gave him pleasure.

How differently to Lueli was he taking his loss !   The reason must be that Lueli though losing his god had kept his faith.   Lueli had lost something real, like losing an umbrella ; he had lost it with frenzy and conviction. But *his* loss was utter and retrospective, a lightning-flash loss which had wiped out a whole life-time of having.   In fact the best way of expressing it, though it sounded silly and paradoxical, was to say that what he had lost for ever was nothing.   ' Forever is a word that stretches backward too,' he explained to himself.   If any proof were needed

his own behaviour was supplying it. He had
ceased to believe in God, but this was making
no difference to him. Consequently what he
had ceased to believe in had never been.

He sighed—the loud horse's sigh of one
who has come to the end of a long stint.
Then he stood up amid the rain and the
ashes and stretched himself. He had got
pins and needles in his leg from sitting still
for so long, but it was a pleasure to his body
to stretch and he stretched once more. The
air struck cold on the muscles and skin which
had, as it were, started to live again. He
felt at once both tired and vigorous. In an
odd way he was feeling rather pleased with
himself, a pleasure that was perhaps the
independent pleasure of his flesh which had
waited patiently around his motionless thinking as a dog waits at the feet of its master
absorbed in writing. The pen is thrown
down rather wantonly, so that the ink may
give a little spurt on to the page that a
moment ago was all the world, that now is
finished and prostrate and floutable. The
master gets up and stretches, the dog gam-
bols round him with congratulation. ' Now
you have come home to your senses again,
now we can be reasonable and go for a walk ! '

He leant down and gave Lueli a little
shake, affectionate but brisk.

' Wake up, wake up. We are going down
to the village now to find a lodging. You
cannot sleep here in the rain all day or you
will get rheumatism.'

A policeman could not have been kinder,
a mother more competent. He had got
Lueli up and walking through the wet
woods and eating stirabout by Ori's fire
before he had had time to bethink him of
his unhappiness.

Lueli sat swallowing and blinking and
looking very debauched and youthful while
Mr. Fortune and Ori made arrangements.
For the present they could live under the
chief's ample roof. Meanwhile the burnt
hut could be rebuilt, or some dwelling could
be fitted up to receive them as lodgers,
whichever Mr. Fortune thought best. As
for the volcano, that would not interfere
with anybody's plans. The pigs had been
corralled once more, the earthquake was
already half-forgotten. Ori had sent an old
woman up to the mountain to make a
reconnaissance, and she had reported that
the lava was flowing down the south side of
the mountain where nobody lived. Every-

thing was all right again, and the rain would freshen things up nicely. To-morrow he would invite a few friends in, and there would be roast meat and a party in honour of his guest.

Personally Mr. Fortune would have preferred to have the former hut rebuilt and to go on living there, much as of old except for religion, the harmonium, and other European amenities. But he feared that Lueli would mope and be miserable. It would be better for him to have a change of scene, company and gaiety. Accordingly, he arranged that for the future they should lodge with Teioa, a lesser chief, whose family included several lively sons and daughters and an extremely vivacious great-grandmother.

Unfortunately this plan worked badly. Mr. Fortune was much happier than he expected to be. He was now engaged in growing a beard, and freed from any obligation to convert his housemates he found their society very agreeable. The great-grandmother was especially good company. She was a celebrated story-teller, and when she had exhausted her stock of scandals about every one in the village she fell back upon legends and fairy-tales. Mr. Fortune was interested to find that many of these were almost word for word the stories of the Old Testament. One hot afternoon as they sat bathing their legs in a pool and waving away the flies from each other she recounted the story of Joseph and his Brethren. Joseph was called Kila and was carried to the land of Egypt in a canoe, but all the familiar characters were there, all the familiar incidents, even to where Kila turned away from the brothers he was threatening to hide the tears which he could no longer keep back. The only variation was in the character of Isaac, who had changed his sex and split into Joseph's mother and aunt. But in truth the change made little difference, nor did it detract from the dignity of the story, for in spite of our English prejudice there is nothing inherently ridiculous about a mother's sister. Mr. Fortune was not perturbed to hear the history of the Jews from the lips of a wrinkled and engraved old Polynesian harridan. He reflected that everywhere mankind is subject to the same anxious burden of love and loneliness, and must in self-defence enchant their cares into a story and a dream. In return for Joseph and his Brethren he told the old dame of the adventures of Mr. Pickwick, many of which were new to her.

But while Mr. Fortune was getting on so nicely Lueli was very unhappy. His play-mates had soon found out his misfortune. They teased him, saying that he had lost his god and would soon go to Hell. Every day the boy grew more dispirited. He shunned his fellows and went slinking off to hide himself in the woods, where he could mope in peace and quiet. Late in the evening he would creep back, smelling of damp forest earth and wild spices ; and without a word he would lie down on his mat and fall into a dreary slumber.

One day Teioa remarked to Mr. Fortune : ' That boy has lost his god. I expect he will die soon.'

' What nonsense ! ' shouted Mr. Fortune in a loud rude voice. He felt too suddenly sick to choose his words. He remembered what he had once read in a book about the Polynesians : that they can renounce life at their own will, not with the splash of suicide, but slowly, sullenly, deliberately, driving death into themselves like a wedge. Was Lueli doing this—gay, inconsequent, casual Lueli ? But since the loss of his god Lueli was gay no longer, and his casualness had taken on a new and terrible aspect, as though it were the casualness of one who could not be bothered to live, who was discarding life as naturally and callously as he had picked flowers and thrown them down to die.

Just then a troop of boys and girls danced by. They were dancing after Lueli and pelting him with small glittering fishes. 'Catch!' they cried; 'here's a god for you, Lueli. Catch him!'

Lueli walked on as if he hadn't noticed them. He looked down and saw one of the fish lying at his feet. Like an animal he picked it up and began eating it, but he ate inattentively, without appetite. He was like a sick dog that snatches listlessly at a tuft of grass. Mr. Fortune stepped out from the verandah. His intention had been to drive the dancers away, but instead of that he put his arm through Lueli's and began walking him down to the beach.

'Let us bathe together,' he said. 'It is a long time since you gave me a swimming-lesson.'

Lueli swam so beautifully that it was hard to believe he was not happy. Mr. Fortune surpassed himself in flounderings. He tried to catch a fish in his mouth.

When they were sitting on the beach again he said : 'Where shall we live when we leave Teioa's house ? Shall we make a new hut or shall we build up our old one again ? '

'Go back to the old,' Lueli replied instantly in a soft fearful whisper.

'Yes, I think so too. Our own bathing-pool is much the best.'

'Yes. It 's deeper than the one here.'

'I think the fish are tamer too.'

'Yes.'

'I was wondering if we couldn't make a small wicker-work bower on a pole and teach the parrots to sleep in it. In England people do so, only the birds are doves, not parrots. Perhaps you remember me telling you about our doves and pigeons ? '

'They take messages.'

'Yes, those are the carrier pigeons. There are also pouters and fantails and tumbling pigeons that turn head over heels in the air. But parrots would be very nice too You could feed them.'

'Won't they be able to feed themselves ? '

'Oh yes, certainly. But they would be more apt to stay with us if we fed them.'

' Must they stay ? '

' Now, am I diverting him from his grief,' thought Mr. Fortune, ' or am I only boring him ? '

The new hut that rose on the place of the old had a faint whiff of burning. Mr. Fortune had superintended the building of it, and because the islanders were fond of him they allowed him to introduce several novelties, such as window-boxes and a kitchen dresser. He also threw out a bay. The parrot-cote stood in a corner of the lawn, and leading up to it was a narrow serpentining path with crazy paving made out of flat shells. On the other side of the house to balance the parrot-cote was a pergola, constructed in bamboo. In front of the house, in fact exactly where it always had been, but uprooted by the earthquake, was the flat stone on which he had celebrated Holy Communion on that first Sunday morning. He looked at it a little sadly. He bore it no malice, although it reminded him of a special kind of happiness which he could taste no more. He decided that he would make it the headstone of a rock-garden.

Mr. Fortune attached special importance to these European refinements because he felt that to the eyes of the world he must now present such an un-European appearance. The earthquake had left him nothing save the clothes he stood up in, the contents of his pockets, and a good-sized rubbish-heap. As for the rubbish-heap, he had with his own hands grubbed a large hole among the bushes and buried therein the bones of the harmonium, lamp, sewing-machine, etc., also the molten images of the communion plate and the teapot. He had done this by night, working by moonlight in the approved fashion of those who have a past to put away, and when he had covered in the hole and stamped down the earth he went back and forth from the ruins to the bushes, scooping up the ashes in a gourd and scattering them in the undergrowth.

His clothes he had folded and put away, thinking that as they were all he had, he had better save them up for future emergencies, such as a shipwreck, a visit of American tourists, the arrival of a new missionary or somebody dropping in from a flying machine. In their stead he wore a kilt and a mantle of native cloth, soberly contrived without any fringes or fandangos, and sandals of plaited bark. Since this new garb was pocketless,

the contents of his pockets were ranged on
the shelf of honour of the kitchen dresser—
a pocket magnifying-glass, a whistle, a nail-
file, a graduated medicine spoon, a flint-and-
steel lighter, a copper medal commemorating
Parnell which Henry Martin had brought
from Ireland as a curiosity, nineteen mother-
of-pearl counters in a wash-leather bag, a
pencil-sharpener blunted by sand getting
into it, a tape-measure that sprang back into
a boxwood nut, several buttons, a silver
pencil-case with no pencil, and a small
magnet painted scarlet. There was also a
knife with two blades, but this he carried
on a string round his neck.

He looked on this array without sentiment.
The parrot-cote and the pergola were also
without charms for him. His intentions
were severely practical. These things were
all part of his designs on Lueli, they were so
many fish-hooks to draw him from despair.
Not by their proper qualities, of course;
Mr. Fortune was not so simple as to expect
that, even of the magnet. But indirectly
they would build up around their owner and
designer a compelling spiritual splendour, a
glamour of mysterious attributes, fastidious
living, and foreign parts. After three years

of such familiarity it would not be easy to reconstruct his first fascination as something rich and strange. But it must be done if he were to compete successfully with his rival in Lueli's affections. It must be done, because that rival was death.

He thought as little as he could help about his progress in this contest. He dared not allow himself to be elated when he seemed to be gaining a little, he dared not admit the possibility of failure. He fought with his eyes turned away from the face of the adversary, like Perseus attacking the Gorgon. He fought by inches, by half-hours ; he dared not attempt a decisive victory for he could not risk a decisive defeat. And when he crept out of the hut at night to refresh himself with solitude and darkness, the sullen red light kindling and wavering above the blackness of the crags betokened to him that his enemy was also awake and weaving his powerful spells of annihilation.

He had no time to think of his own loss. He was entirely taken up with solicitude for Lueli, a soul no longer—as he supposed— immortal, and for that reason a charge upon him all the more urgent, as one is more concerned for a humming-bird than for a tortoise. Only at such times as when he had received a serious set-back or was feeling especially desperate did he find himself on the point of taking refuge in prayer ; and then remembering the real state of things he would feel exactly like a person who makes to cast himself down on a chair but recalls just in time (or maybe just too late) how all the furniture has been moved, and that the chair is no longer in its old place.

It was sometimes hard for him with his English prejudices not to grow irritated at Lueli's abject listlessness and misery. He could not have believed that his friend could be so chicken-hearted. And since when one is down everything falls on one, circumstances seemed to conspire in twitting and outraging the luckless youth.

Mr. Fortune thought he would try games. Lueli was agile and dexterous, surely it would comfort him to exhibit those qualities. Mr. Fortune introduced him to ping-pong. They played with basket-work bats and small nuts. On the second day a nut hit Lueli and made his nose bleed. He turned green, cast down his bat and began to whimper.

Since ping-pong was too rough, what

about spillikins ? He carved a set of pieces
out of splinters, dyed them with fruit juice to
make them look more appetising, and made a
great show of excitement to tempt the other
on. Whenever it was Lueli's turn to hook a
piece from the tangle he sighed and groaned
as though he had been requested to move
mountains. Dicing and skittles were no
better received.

Deciding that neither games nor gaming
(they diced for the mother-of-pearl counters)
were likely to rouse Lueli from his dejection,
Mr. Fortune cast about for some new ex-
pedient. Perhaps a pet animal might have
charms ? He caught a baby flying fox and
reared it with great tenderness on guavas
and coco-milk. The flying fox soon grew
extremely attached to him and learnt to put
its head out of the cage when he called
' Tibby ! ' But whenever Lueli could be
induced to take an interest in it and to prod
it up with a cautious finger, it scratched and
bit him. Still persevering with natural
history Mr. Fortune spat on the magnifying-
glass, polished it, and began to show off the
wonderful details of flowers, mosses, and
water-fleas. Lueli would look, and look
away again, obediently and haplessly bored.

Though the idea of such cold and rapacious blood-thirstiness was highly repugnant to him, he resolved to sacrifice his own feelings (and theirs) and make a moth collection. He prepared a mess of honey and water and took Lueli out that evening on an expedition to lime the trees. Two hours later they went out again with a string of candle-nuts for a lantern and collected a quantity of moths and nocturnal insects, poignantly beautiful and battered with their struggles to escape. But he stifled his sense of shame, all the more in that Lueli seemed inclined to rise to this lure, of his own accord suggesting a second expedition. He had not quite grasped the theory, however. Two days later Mr. Fortune, returning from an errand in the village, was surprised to hear a loud and furious buzzing proceeding from the dell. It was full of wild bees, and Lueli, very swollen and terrified, came crawling out of the bushes. He had smeared the parrot-cote and the posts of the verandah with honey, and it seemed as though every bee and wasp on the island were assembled together to quarrel and gorge themselves. It was not possible to approach the hut until after nightfall, and drunk and disorderly

bees hovered about it for days, not to speak
of a sediment of ants.

Worse was to come. Since his arrival on
the island Mr. Fortune had never ailed.
But now, whether by exposure to night dews
and getting his feet damp out mothing or by
some special malignity of Fate, he found
himself feeling sore at the back of the throat
and sneezing; and presently he had de-
veloped a streaming cold. Lueli caught it
from him, and if his cold were bad, Lueli's
was ten times worse. He made no effort to
struggle against it; indeed, he was so over-
whelmed that struggling was practically out
of the question. He crouched on his mats,
snorting and groaning, with a face all
chapped and bloated, blear eyes, a hanging
jaw, and a sullen and unhealthy appetite;
and every five minutes or so he sneezed as
though he would bring the roof down.

Mr. Fortune was terrified, not only for
Lueli, but for the whole population of the
island. He knew how direly European
diseases can rampage through a new field.
He set up a rigid quarantine. Since the loss
of his god Lueli had been at pains to avoid
his friends, but naturally he was now seized
with a passionate craving for their society;

and there was some excuse for him, as Mr. Fortune was not just now very exhilarating company. But he did his best to be, in spite of an earache which followed the cold, and between Lueli's paroxysms of sneezing he strove to cheer him with accounts of the Great Plague and the Brave Men of Eyam.

At last they were both recovered. But though restored in body Lueli was as mopish as ever. Mr. Fortune went on bracing, and beat his brains for some new distraction. But he had lost ground in this last encounter, and the utmost he could congratulate himself upon was that Lueli was still, however indifferently or unwillingly, consenting to exist. The worst of it was that he couldn't allow himself to show any sympathy. There were times when he could scarcely hold himself back from pity and condolence. But he believed that if he were once to acknowledge the other's grief he would lose his greatest hold over him—his title of being some one superior, august and exemplary.

And then one morning, when they had been living in the new hut for about six weeks, he woke up inspired. Why had he wasted so much time displaying his most trivial and uncompelling charms, opposing to the magnetism of death such fripperies and titbits of this world, such gewgaws of civilisation as a path serpentining to a parrot-cote (a parrot-cote which hadn't even allured the parrots), or a pocket magnifying-glass, while all the time he carried within him the inestimable treasures of intellectual enjoyment? Now he would pipe Lueli a tune worth dancing to, now he would open for him a new world. He would teach him mathematics.

He sprang up from bed, full of enthusiasm. At the thought of all those stretches of white beach he was like a bridegroom. There they were, hard and smooth from the tread of the sea, waiting for that noble consummation of blank surfaces, to show forth a truth ; waiting, in this particular instance, to show forth the elements of plane geometry.

At breakfast Mr. Fortune was so glorified and gay that Lueli caught a reflection of his high spirits and began to look more lifelike than he had done for weeks. On their way down to the beach they met a party of islanders who were off on a picnic. Mr. Fortune with delight heard Lueli answering their greetings with something like his former sociability, and even plucking up heart enough for a repartee. His delight gave a momentary stagger when Lueli decided to go a-picnicking too. But, after all, it didn't matter a pin. The beach would be as smooth again to-morrow, the air as sweet and nimble ; Lueli would be in better trim for learning after a spree, and, now he came to think of it, he himself wouldn't teach any the worse for a little private rubbing-up beforehand.

It must be going on for forty years since he had done any mathematics ; for he had gone into the bank the same year that his father died, leaving Rugby at seventeen because, in the state that things were then in, the bank was too good an opening to be missed. He had once got a prize—the Poetical Works of Longfellow—for algebra, and he had scrambled along well enough in other branches of mathematics ; but he had not learnt with any particular thrill, or realised that thrill there might be, until he was in the bank, and learning a thing of the past.

Then, perhaps because of that never-ending entering and adding up and striking balances, and turning on to the next page to enter, add up, and strike balances again, a mental occupation minute, immediate, and yet, so to speak, wool-gathering, as he imagined knitting to be, the absolute quality of mathematics began to take on for him an inexpressibly romantic air. ' Pure Mathematics.' He used to speak of them to his fellow-clerks as though he were hinting at some kind of transcendental debauchery of which he had been made free—and indeed there does seem to be a kind of unnatural vice in being so completely pure. After a spell of this holy boasting he would grow a little uneasy ; and going to the Free Library he took out mathematical treatises, just to make sure that he could follow step by step as well as soar. For twenty pages, perhaps, he read slowly, carefully, dutifully, with pauses for self-examination and working out the examples. Then, just as it was working up and the pauses should have been more scrupulous than ever, a kind of swoon and ecstasy would fall on him, and he read ravening on, sitting up till dawn to finish the book, as though it were a novel. After that his passion was stayed ; the book went back to the Library and he was done with mathematics till the next bout. Not much remained with him after these orgies, but something remained : a sensation in the mind, a worshipping acknowledgment of something isolated and unassailable, or a remembered mental joy at the rightness of thoughts coming together to a conclusion, accurate thoughts, thoughts in just intonation, coming together like unaccompanied voices coming to a close.

But often his pleasure flowered from quite simple things that any fool could grasp. For instance, he would look out of the bank windows, which had green shades in their lower halves ; and rising above the green shades he would see a row of triangles, equilateral, isosceles, acute-angled, right-angled, obtuse-angled. These triangles were a range of dazzling mountain peaks, eternally snowy, eternally untrodden ; and he could feel the keen wind which blew from their summits. Yet they were also a row of triangles, equilateral, isosceles, acute-angled, right-angled, obtuse-angled.

This was the sort of thing he designed for Lueli's comfort. Geometry would be much better than algebra, though he had not the same certificate from Longfellow for teaching it. Algebra is always dancing over the pit of the unknown, and he had no wish to direct Lueli's thoughts to that quarter. Geometry would be best to begin with, plain plane geometry, immutably plane. Surely if anything could minister to the mind diseased it would be the steadfast contemplation of a right angle, an existence that no mist of human tears could blur, no blow of fate deflect.

Walking up and down the beach, admiring the surface which to-morrow with so much epiphany and glory was going to reveal the first axioms of Euclid, Mr. Fortune began to think of himself as possessing an universal elixir and charm. A wave of missionary ardour swept him along, and he seemed to view, not Lueli only, but all the islanders rejoicing in this new dispensation. There was beach-board enough for all and to spare. The picture grew in his mind's eye, somewhat indebted to Raphael's Cartoon of the School of Athens. Here a group bent over an equation, there they pointed out to each other with admiration that the square on the hypotenuse equalled the sum of the squares on the sides containing the right angle; here was one delighting in a rhomboid and another in conic sections; that enraptured figure had secured the twelfth root of two, while the children might be filling up the foreground with a little long division.

By the morrow he had slept off most of his fervour. Calm, methodical, with a mind prepared for the onset, he guided Lueli down to the beach and with a stick prodded a small hole in it.

' What is this ? '

' A hole.'

' No, Lueli, it may seem like a hole, but it is a point.'

Perhaps he had prodded a little too emphatically. Lueli's mistake was quite natural. Anyhow, there were bound to be a few misunderstandings at the start.

He took out his pocket-knife and whittled the end of the stick. Then he tried again.

' What is this ? '

' A smaller hole.'

' Point,' said Mr. Fortune suggestively.

' Yes, I mean a smaller point.'

' No, not quite. It is a point, but it is not smaller. Holes may be of different sizes, but no point is larger or smaller than another point.'

Lueli looked from the first point to the second. He seemed to be about to speak, but to think better of it. He removed his gaze to the sea.

Meanwhile Mr. Fortune had moved about, prodding more points. It was rather awkward that he should have to walk on the beach-board, for his footmarks distracted the eye from the demonstration.

' Look, Lueli ! '

Lueli turned his gaze inland.

' Where ? ' said he.

' At all these. Here ; and here ; and here. But don't tread on them.'

Lueli stepped back hastily. When he was well out of the danger zone he stood looking at Mr. Fortune with great attention and some uneasiness.

' These are all points.'

Lueli recoiled a step further. Standing on one leg he furtively inspected the sole of his foot.

' As you see, Lueli, these points are in different places. This one is to the west of that, and consequently that one is to the east of this. Here is one to the south. Here are two close together, and there is one quite apart from all the others. Now look at them, remember what I have said, think carefully, and tell me what you think.'

Inclining his head and screwing up his eyes Lueli inspected the demonstration with an air of painstaking connoisseurship. At length he ventured the opinion that the hole lying apart from the others was perhaps the neatest. But if Mr. Fortune would give him the knife he would whittle the stick even finer.

' Now what did I tell you ? Have you forgotten that points cannot be larger or smaller ? If they were holes it would be a different matter. But these are points. Will you remember that ? '

Lueli nodded. He parted his lips, he was about to ask a question. Mr. Fortune went on hastily.

' Now suppose I were to cover the whole beach with these ; what then ? '

A look of dismay came over Lueli's countenance. Mr. Fortune withdrew the hypothesis.

' I don't intend to. I only ask you to imagine what it would be like if I did.'

The look of dismay deepened.

' They would all be points,' said Mr. Fortune impressively. ' All in different places. And none larger or smaller than another.

' What I have explained to you is summed

up in the axiom : a point has position but not magnitude. In other words, if a given point were not in a given place it would not be there at all.'

Whilst allowing time for this to sink in he began to muse about those other words. Were they quite what he meant ? Did they indeed mean anything ? Perhaps it would have been better not to try to supplement Euclid. He turned to his pupil. The last words had sunk in at any rate, had been received without scruple and acted upon. Lueli was out of sight.

Compared with his intentions, actuality had been a little quelling. It became more quelling as time went on. Lueli did not again remove himself without leave ; he soon discovered that Mr. Fortune was extremely in earnest, and was resigned to regular instruction every morning and a good deal of rubbing-in and evocation during the rest of the day. No one ever had a finer capacity for listening than he, or a more docile and obliging temperament. But whereas in the old days these good gifts had flowed from him spontaneously and pleasurably, he now seemed to be exhibiting them by rote and in a manner almost desperate, as though he were listening and obliging as a circus animal does its tricks. Humane visitors to circuses often point out with what alacrity the beasts run into the ring to perform their turn. They do not understand that in the choice of two evils most animals would rather flourish round a spacious ring than be shut up in a cage. The activity and the task is a distraction from their unnatural lot, and they tear through paper hoops all the better because so much of their time is spent behind iron bars.

It had been a very different affair when Lueli was learning Bible history and the Church Catechism, *The King of Love my Shepherd is* and *The Old Hundredth.* Then there had been no call for this blatant submission ; lessons had been an easy-going conversation, with Lueli keeping his end up as an intelligent pupil should and Mr. Fortune feeling like a cross between wise old Chiron and good Mr. Barlow. Now they were a succession of harangues, and rather strained harangues to boot. Theology, Mr. Fortune found, is a more accommodating subject than mathematics ; its technique of exposition allows greater latitude. For instance, when you are gravelled for matter there is always the moral to fall back upon. Comparisons too may be drawn, leading cases cited, types and antetypes analysed, and anecdotes introduced. Except for Archimedes, mathematics is singularly naked of anecdotes.

Not that he thought any the worse of it for this. On the contrary he compared its austere and integral beauty to theology decked out in her flaunting charms and wielding all her bribes and spiritual bonuses ; and like Dante at the rebuke of Beatrice he blushed that he should ever have followed aught but the noblest. No, there was nothing lacking in mathematics. The deficiency was in him. He added line to line, precept to precept ; he exhausted himself and his pupil by hours of demonstration and exposition ; leagues of sand were scarred, and smoothed again by the tide, and scarred afresh : never an answering spark rewarded him. He might as well have made the sands into a rope-walk.

Sometimes he thought that he was taxing Lueli too heavily, and desisted. But if he desisted for pity's sake, pity soon drove him to work again, for if it were bad to see Lueli sighing over the properties of parallel lines, it was worse to see him moping and pining for his god. Teioa's words, uttered so matter-of-factly, haunted his mind. ' I expect he will die soon.' Mr. Fortune was thinking so too. Lueli grew steadily more lack-lustre, his eyes were dull, his voice was flat ; he appeared to be retreating behind a film that thickened and toughened and would soon obliterate him.

' If only, if only I could teach him to enjoy an abstract notion ! If he could once grasp how it all hangs together, and is everlasting and harmonious, he would be saved. Nothing else can save him, nothing that I or his fellows can offer him. For it must be new to excite him and it must be true to hold him, and what else is there that is both new and true ? '

There were women, of course, a race of beings neither new nor true, yet much vaunted by some as a cure for melancholy and a tether for the soul. Mr. Fortune would have cheerfully procured a damsel (not that they were likely to need much of that), dressed her hair, hung the whistle and the Parnell medal round her neck, dowered her with the nineteen counters and the tape-measure, and settled her in Lueli's bed

if he had supposed that this would avail.
But he feared that Lueli was past the
comfort of women, and in any case that
sort of thing is best arranged by the parties
concerned.

So he resorted to geometry again, and
once more Lueli was hurling himself with
frantic docility through the paper hoops. It
was really rather astonishing how dense he
could be ! Once out of twenty, perhaps, he
would make the right answer. Mr. Fortune,
too anxious to be lightly elated, would probe
a little into his reasons for making it. Either
they were the wrong reasons or he had no
reasons at all. Mr. Fortune was often
horribly tempted to let a mistake pass. He
was not impatient—he was far more patient
than in the palmiest days of theology—but
he found it almost unendurable to be for
ever saying with various inflections of kindness : 'No, Lueli. Try again'; or : 'Well,
no, not exactly'; or : 'I fear you have not
quite understood'; or : 'Let me try to make
that clearer.' He withstood the temptation.
His easy acceptance (though in good faith)
of a sham had brought them to this pass, and
tenderness over a false currency was not
likely to help them out of it. No, he would

not be caught that way twice. Similarly he pruned and repressed Lueli's talent for leaking away down side-issues, though this was hard too, for it involved snubbing him almost every time he spoke on his own initiative.

Just as he had been so mistaken about the nature of points, confounding them with holes and agitating himself at the prospect of a beach pitted all over, Lueli contrived to apply the same sort of well-meaning misconceptions to every stage of his progress— if progress be the word to apply to one who is hauled along in a state of semi-consciousness by the scruff of his neck. When the points seemed to be tolerably well established in his mind Mr. Fortune led him on to lines, and by joining up points he illustrated such simple figures as the square, the triangle, and the parallelogram. Lueli perked up, seemed interested, borrowed the stick and began joining up points too. At first he copied Mr. Fortune, glancing up after each stroke to see if it had been properly directed. Then growing rather more confident, and pleased —as who is not?—with the act of drawing on sand, he launched out into a more complicated design.

'This is a man,' he said.

Mr. Fortune was compelled to reply coldly :

' A man is not a geometrical figure.'

At length Mr. Fortune decided that he had better take in sail. Pure mathematics were obviously beyond Lueli ; perhaps applied mathematics would work better. Mr. Fortune, as it happened, had never applied any, but he knew that other people did so, and though he considered it a rather lower line of business he was prepared to try it.

' If I were to ask you to find out the height of that tree, how would you set about it ? '

Lueli replied with disconcerting readiness :

' I should climb up to the top and let down a string.'

' But suppose you couldn't climb up it ? '

' Then I should cut it down.'

' That would be very wasteful ; and the other way might be dangerous. I can show you a better plan than either of those.'

The first thing was to select a tree, an upright tree, because in all elementary demonstrations it is best to keep things as clear as possible. He would never have credited the rarity of upright trees had he not been pressed to find one. Coco-palms, of course, were hopeless : they all had a curve or a list. At length he remembered a tree near the bathing-pool, a perfect specimen of everything a tree should be, tall, straight as a die, growing by itself ; set apart, as it were, for purposes of demonstration.

He marched Lueli thither, and when he saw him rambling towards the pool he recalled him with a cough.

' Now I will show you how to discover the height of that tree. Attend. You will find it very interesting. The first thing to do is to lie down.'

Mr. Fortune lay down on his back and Lueli followed his example.

Many people find that they can think more clearly in a recumbent position. Mr. Fortune found it so too. No sooner was he on his back than he remembered that he had no measuring-stick. But the sun was delicious and the grass soft ; he might well spare a few minutes in exposing the theory.

' It is all a question of measurements. Now my height is six foot two inches, but for the sake of argument we will assume it to be six foot exactly. The distance from my eye to the base of the tree is so far an unknown quantity. My six feet, however, are already known to you.'

Now Lueli had sat up, and was looking him up and down with an intense and curious scrutiny, as though he were something utterly unfamiliar. This was confusing, it made him lose the thread of his explanation. He felt a little uncertain as to how it should proceed.

Long ago, on dark January mornings, when a septic thumb (bestowed on him by a cat which he had rescued from a fierce poodle) obliged him to stay away from the bank, he had observed young men with woollen comforters and raw-looking wind-bitten hands practising surveying under the snarling elms and whimpering poplars of Finsbury Park. They had tapes and tripods, and the girls in charge of perambulators dawdled on the asphalt paths to watch their proceedings. It was odd how vividly frag-ments of his old life had been coming back to him during these last few months.

He resumed :

' In order to ascertain the height of the tree I must be in such a position that the top of the tree is exactly in a line with the top of a measuring-stick—or any straight object would do, such as an umbrella—which I shall secure in an upright position between my feet. Knowing then that the ratio that the height of the tree bears to the length of the measuring-stick must equal the ratio that the distance from my eye to the base of the tree bears to my height, and knowing (or being able to find out) my height, the length of the measuring-stick, and the distance from my eye to the base of the tree, I can, therefore, calculate the height of the tree.'

' What is an umbrella ? '

Again the past flowed back, insurgent and actual. He was at the Oval, and out of an overcharged sky it had begun to rain again. In a moment the insignificant tapestry of lightish faces was exchanged for a noble pattern of domes, blackish, blueish, and greenish domes, sprouting like a crop of miraculous and religious mushrooms. The rain fell harder and harder, presently the little-white figures were gone from the field and, as with an abnegation of humanity, the green plain, so much smaller for their departure, lay empty and forsaken, ringed round with tier upon tier of blackly glistening umbrellas.

He longed to describe it all to Lueli, it seemed to him at the moment that he could talk with the tongues of angels about umbrellas. But this was a lesson in mathematics : applied mathematics moreover, a compromise, so that all further compromises must be sternly nipped. Unbending to no red herrings, he replied :

'An umbrella, Lueli, when in use resembles the—the shell that would be formed by rotating an arc of curve about its axis of symmetry, attached to a cylinder of small radius whose axis is the same as the axis of symmetry of the generating curve of the shell. When not in use it is properly an elongated cone, but it is more usually helicoidal in form.'

Lueli made no answer. He lay down again, this time face downward.

Mr. Fortune continued : 'An umbrella, however, is not essential. A stick will do just as well, so find me one, and we will go on to the actual measurement.'

Lueli was very slow in finding a stick. He looked for it rather languidly and stupidly, but Mr. Fortune tried to hope that this was because his mind was engaged on what he had just learnt.

Holding the stick between his feet, Mr. Fortune wriggled about on his back trying to get into the proper position. He knew he was making a fool of himself. The young

men in Finsbury Park had never wriggled
about on their backs. Obviously there
must be some more dignified way of getting
the top of the stick in line with the top of the
tree and his eye, but just then it was not
obvious to him. Lueli made it worse by
standing about and looking miserably on.
When he had placed himself properly he
remembered that he had not measured the
stick. It measured (he had had the fore-
thought to bring the tape with him) three
foot seven, very tiresome—those odd inches
would only serve to make it seem harder to
his pupil. So he broke it again, drove it into
the ground, and wriggled on his stomach
till his eye was in the right place, which was
a slight improvement in method at any rate.
He then handed the tape to Lueli, and lay
strictly motionless, admonishing and direct-
ing, while Lueli did the measuring of the
ground. In the interests of accuracy he did
it thrice, each time with a different result.
A few minutes before noon the height of the
tree was discovered to be fifty-seven foot
nine inches.

Mr. Fortune now had leisure for com-
passion. He thought Lueli was looking hot
and fagged, so he said :

' Why don't you have a bathe ? It will freshen you up.'

Lueli raised his head and looked at him with a long dubious look, as though he had heard the words but without understanding what they meant. Then he turned his eyes to the tree and looked at that. A sort of shadowy wrinkle, like the blurring on the surface of milk before it boils, crossed his face.

' Don't worry any more about that tree. If you hate all this so much we won't do any more of it, I will never speak of geometry again. Put it all out of your head and go and bathe.'

Still Lueli looked at him as though he heard but didn't understand. Then in the same sleep-walking fashion he turned and went down towards the bathing-pool.

Presently, looking between the trees, Mr. Fortune saw him reappear on the rock above the deep part of the pool. He was going to dive. Very slowly and methodically he took off everything that was on him, he even took off his earrings. Then he stretched his arms in a curve above his head and leapt in.

A beautiful dive—Mr. Fortune found himself thinking of the arc of a stretched bow, the curve and flash of a scimitar, the jet of a harpoon—all instruments of death, all displaying the same austere and efficient kind of beauty, the swiftness to shed blood. A beautiful dive—and a long one. Had he come up already ? Hardly ; for from where he sat Mr. Fortune could see almost the whole surface of the bathing-pool. Perhaps, though, he had come up behind the rock, swimming back under water.

Mr. Fortune rose to his feet. Instantly, with the movement, agonising fear took hold of him. He ran down to the pool, and out along the rocks, shouting and calling. No sign, only the quietly heaving water under the impervious blue sky. No sound, except the parrots and sea-birds squawking in answer to his disturbing voice. Lueli was staying down on purpose. He was holding on to the seaweed, drowning himself, with the resolute fatal despair of his light-hearted race.

Mr. Fortune leapt over his own fear of deep water. Where Lueli had dived he could dive too. He hurled himself off the rock, he felt the water break like a stone under him, he felt himself smothered and sinking ; and the next moment he was bouncing about on the surface, utterly and hopelessly afloat. He kicked and beat the water, trying to force a passage downward. It would not let him through.

He swam to the rock and scrambled out into the weight of air and dived for a second time. Once more the sea caught him and held him up.

' Damn ! ' he said, softly and swiftly, as though he were pursuing a pencil which had rolled into a dark corner out of reach.

Since diving was out of the question he must run to the village to fetch helpers. The village was nearly a mile away, there might be no one there but old women and babies, he would be breathless, every one would shout and wave their arms, by the time he got back with a rescue party it would be too late, Lueli would be drowned.

This time it was harder to haul himself out of the water, for he had forgotten to throw off his large draperies and they were now water-logged. After the shadow of the pool the sunlight seemed black and blinding. He started to run, loosening the knots as he went, for he would run quicker naked. As he threw off the cloak he caught sight over his shoulder of a canoe out to sea. It was heading away from the island, but perhaps it was still within earshot. He shouted and waved the cloak and shouted and coo-eed again. Each cry came out of his body like a thing with jagged edges, tearing him inwardly. The canoe kept on its course. The sweat ran down and blinded him, so that he thought for a moment that the canoe had changed its direction and was coming towards him : but it was only the sweat in his eyes which had enlarged it.

He began to run again. It was a pity that he had wasted so much good breath shouting. He was among the trees now, rushing down a vista of light and shadow. Each tall tree seemed to gather speed as he approached it till it shot past him with a whirr of foliage and a swoop of darkness. His going shook the ground, and the fruit fell off the bushes as he ran by.

The path began to wind downhill and grew stonier. He was about half-way to the village, he could hear the noise of the brook. He shot round a corner, tripped over something, and fell headlong into a group of human beings, falling among smooth brown limbs and cries of astonishment. It was one of those bevies, half a dozen young women who had come out to the brook to net crayfish. To his horror they all leapt to their feet and began to run away. Lying along the ground as he fell, with his head in the brook, he caught hold of an ankle.

' Stop ! Don't be little fools ! ' he cried out, sobbing for breath. ' Lueli is drowning in the bathing-pool. You must come back with me and save him.'

The ankle belonged to Fuma, a hoyden whom he had once loathed beyond words ; but now he adored her, for she was going to play up. She called back the other girls, rallied them, sent one back to the village, and bade the others run as fast as they could to the pool ; and in a twinkling she and Mr. Fortune were following them up through the woods. Fuma caught hold of his arm and patted it encouragingly.

' He is in the deep hole under the black rock,' he said. ' He is lying there holding on to the weed. I have been shouting, and I may not be able to keep up with you. But you must run on without me and dive until you find him.'

' Silly boy ! Silly Lueli ! He told me three days ago that he meant to die. Such nonsense ! Never mind, we will pull him up and breathe him alive again.'

They ran on side by side. Presently Mr. Fortune said : 'You know, Fuma, this is all my fault.'

Fuma laughed under her breath. 'Lueli thinks the world of you,' she said. 'He is always telling us how lovable you are.'

After a few more yards Mr. Fortune said : 'Fuma, you must run on alone now.'

She gave his arm a gentle nip and shot ahead. He saw her join the others as a starling flies into the flock, and then they were out of sight. He could only think of quite small immediate things, Fuma's eyebrows, a beautiful clear arch, and the soft quick sound of her breathing. He was thinking more of her than of Lueli. She seemed more real.

He was still running, but now every time that he put a foot down it was with a stamp that disintegrated his balance, so that he could not guide his direction. Then he heard a splash, and another and another. They had reached the pool and begun diving. Then he heard Fuma's voice crying : 'Further to the left. He's down here.' Then a babble of voices and more splashings. Then silence.

He gathered up his will for the last thirty

yards, was down on to the beach and out breast high into the water. He saw a girl's head rise above the surface of the empty pool. She shook the hair from her eyes, saw him standing there, and came swimming towards him.

' We 've got him,' she said. ' But Fuma has to cut the weed with a shell for we can't loosen his hands.'

Mr. Fortune took the pocket-knife from his neck and held it out to her. Then he saw a strangely intricate and beautiful group emerge and slowly approach. They had brought up Lueli and were bearing him among them. His head lolled and dipped back into the water from Fuma's shoulder where it lay. His eyes were open in a fixed and piteous stare, his mouth was open too, and a little trickle of blood ran down from his lip where he had bitten it. His inanimate body trailed in the water with gestures inexpressibly weary. But two long streamers of weed still hung from his clenched hands.

Death comes with her black ruler and red ink and scores a firm line under the long tale of more or less, debit and credit, all the small multitudinous entries which have made up the relationship between one's self and another. The line is drawn, the time has come to audit ; and from the heart of her shadow a strange clarity, dream-like and precise, is shed upon the page, so that without any doubt or uncertainty we can add up the account which is now at an end, and perceive the sum-total of the expenditure of time. While the others were ministering around the body of Lueli, squeezing the water out of his lungs, rubbing him, breathing into his nostrils, burning herbs and performing incantations, Mr. Fortune sat under a tree, a little apart, and audited the past. In the tree sat a parrot, uttering from time to time its curious airy whistle—a high, sweet, meditative note. It seemed to Mr. Fortune that the bird was watching the process of his thoughts, and that its whistle, detached from any personal emotion, even from that of astonishment, was an involuntary and philosophic acknowledgment of the oddity of men's lives and passions.

'I loved him,' he thought. 'From the moment I set eyes on him I loved him. Not with what is accounted a criminal love, for though I set my desire on him it was a spiritual desire. I did not even love him as a father loves a son, for that is a familiar love, and at the times when Lueli most entranced me it was as a being remote, intact, and incalculable. I waited to see what his next movement would be, if he would speak or no —it was the not knowing what he would do that made him dear. Yes, that was how I loved him best, those were my happiest moments : when I was just aware of him, and sat with my senses awaiting him, not wishing to speak, not wishing to make him notice me until he did so of his own accord because no other way would it be perfect, would it be by him. And how often, I wonder, have I let it be just like that ? Perhaps a dozen times, perhaps twenty times all told, perhaps, when all is put together, for an hour out of the three years I have had with him. For man's will is a demon that will not let him be. It leads him to the edge of a clear pool ; and while he sits admiring it, with his soul suspended over it like a green branch and dwelling in its own reflection, will stretches out his hand and closes his fingers upon a stone—a stone to throw into it.

' I 'd had a poor, meagre, turnpike sort of

life until I came here and found Lueli. I loved him, he was a refreshment to me, my only pleasant surprise. He was perfect because he *was* a surprise. I had done nothing to win him, he was entirely gratuitous. I had had no hand in him, I could no more have imagined him beforehand than I could have imagined a new kind of flower. So what did I do ? I started interfering. I made him a Christian, or thought I did. I taught him to do this and not to do the other, I checked him, I fidgeted over him. And because I loved him so for what he was I could not spend a day without trying to alter him. How dreadful it is that because of our wills we can never love anything without messing it about ! We couldn't even love a tree, not a stone even ; for sooner or later we should be pruning the tree or chipping a bit off the stone. Yet if it were not for a will I suppose we should cease to exist. Anyhow it is in us, and while we live we cannot escape from it, so however we love and whatever we love, it can only be for a few minutes, and to buy off our will for those few minutes we have to relinquish to it for the rest of our lives whatever it is we love. Lueli has been the price of Lueli. I enslaved him, I kept him on a string. I robbed him of his god twice over—first in intention, then in fact. I made his misery more miserable by my perpetual interference. Up till an hour ago I was actually tormenting him with that damned geometry. And now he is dead. . . . Yes, parrot ! You may well whistle. But be careful. Don't attract my attention too much lest I should make a pet of you, and put you in a cage, and then in the end, when you had learnt to talk like me instead of whistling like a wise bird, wring your neck because you couldn't learn to repeat *Paradise Lost.*'

At these words the parrot flew away, just as though it had understood and wished to keep on the safe side ; and looking up Mr. Fortune saw some of the islanders running towards him. He got up and went to meet them. ' Well, is he dead ? ' he asked, too deeply sunk in his own wanhope to pay any attention to their looks and greetings.

It was some time before they could make him understand that Lueli was alive. He followed them, dumb, trembling, and stupefied, to where Lueli was sitting propped up under a tree. He looked rather battered, and rather bewildered, and slightly ashamed of himself, like a child that has been at a rich tea-party, grown over-excited and been sick. But the hag-ridden look he had worn since the earthquake was gone, and he was answering the congratulations and chaff of those around him with a semblance of his old gaiety.

Mr. Fortune stood looking down on him in silence, confused at meeting him whom he had not thought to meet again. Lueli was infected by his embarrassment, and the two regarded each other with caution and constraint, as dear friends do who meet unexpectedly after long separation. Lueli was the first to speak.

'How ill you look. Your face is all holes.'

'Lueli, you would have laughed if you could have seen me trying to dive in after you. Twice I threw myself in, but I could do nothing but float.'

'I expect you let yourself crumple up.'

'Yes, I expect I did.'

'But it was very kind of you to try.'

'Not at all.'

The situation was horrible. Mr. Fortune was tongue-tied, very jealous of the others, and haunted with the feeling that behind all this cause for rejoicing there was some fatal obstacle which he ought to know all about but which his mind was shirking the contemplation of. Lueli fidgeted and made faces. The awkwardness of being raised from the dead was too much even for his *savoir faire*.

' Why can't I be natural ? ' thought Mr. Fortune. ' Why can't I say how glad I feel ? And why don't I feel my gladness ? What have I done ? Why is it like this, what is the matter with me ? '

Lueli's thoughts were something like this : ' He has a blemish on his neck, but didn't I ever notice it before ? It must have grown larger. I hope they won't begin to laugh at him because he can't dive. I love him, but, oh dear ! what a responsibility he is. I don't think I can bear it much longer, not just now. I don't want responsibilities. I only want to go to sleep.'

Round them stood half the population of the island, raging with congratulations, jokes, and inquiries. Even when they had escorted them back to the hut, superintended Lueli's falling asleep, and eaten all the provisions which Mr. Fortune brought out to

them, they would not go away but sat among
their crumbs and on the rock-garden imploring Fuma to tell them once more how
Mr. Fortune had come bounding through
the wood and fallen headlong into the
girls' laps.

For no reason that he could see he had
suddenly become immensely popular. And
as he walked to and fro in the twilight waiting for his guests to take themselves off he
heard his name being bandied about in
tones of the liveliest affection and approval.
He had one consolation : by the morrow he
would be out of fashion again. As for Lueli,
they scarcely mentioned him. If he had
been drowned they would have spent the
evening wailing and lamenting : not for
him but for themselves, at the reminder of
their own mortality, after the natural way
of mourning. And there would have been
just as much gusto, he thought—but tenderly,
for he felt no animosity to them now, only a
desire to get rid of them and be left to his
own soul—and just as many crumbs.

The moon had set before they went away.
Mr. Fortune stole into the hut and listened
for a while to Lueli's quiet breathing, a slight
human rhythm recovered that day from the

rhythm of the sea. He knelt down very quietly and creakingly, and taking hold of Lueli's limp warm hand he put it to his lips. ' Good-bye, my dear,' he murmured under his breath. Lueli stirred, and uttered a drowsy inarticulate Good-night.

Both rhythms were in Mr. Fortune's ears as he lay down to rest. He did not sleep, at least not for some hours ; but he lay un-harried in a solemn and dream-like repose, listening to the gentle fanning of Lueli's slumber and the slow tread of the sea.

Thus, tranquil and full of long thoughts, he had lain on his first night in Fanua, gazing at the star Canopus and watching the trail of creeper stir at the sweet breath of night. All that he had then of hope and faith was lost. But now at the last he seemed strangely to have resumed the temper of that night, and the thought of his renunciation was as full and perfect as the former thought of his vocation had been. ' It is not one's beliefs that matter,' he told himself, ' but to be acting up to them. To have come to Fanua and now to have made up my mind to go away—it is the decision that fills me with this amazing kind of joy.'

To go away. It was the only solution, he

had the parrot's word for it. The slow tread
of the sea told him the same story. ' I
brought you here,' it said, ' and presently
I shall bear you away. My ebbing tides
will return to Fanua, and ebb and return
again and ebb and return again. But for
you there will be no return.' And the tread
of the sea became the footfall of a warder.
It was this necessity, still implicit and un-
realised, which had lain like a stone in his
heart when he saw Lueli brought back from
the dead. If he had not thought of Lueli as
being dead he would never have understood. But Death had vouchsafed him a
beam of her darkness to see clearly by ; and
having seen, he could not sin against that
light. He must go away, that was the only
stratagem by which love could outwit its own
inherent treachery. If he stayed on, flattering himself with the belief that he had learnt
his lesson, he would remember for a while
no doubt ; but sooner or later, inevitably he
would yield to his will again, he would begin
to meddle, he would seek to destroy.

To see everything so clearly and to know
that his mind was made up was almost to be
released from human bondage. This must
be the boasted calm joy of mathematicians

which he had once pretended to share. Euclid had failed him, or he had failed Euclid ; but the contemplation of his own reasoning and resolved mind gave him a felicity beyond even that which the rightness of right-angles could afford. He would keep awake a little longer and make the most of it. He could be sure it would not last. But when it had shattered and desolation came in its stead there would still be common sense and common manliness and several practical preoccupations with which to keep desolation at bay.

First he must get a message to St. Fabien. In the pocket of the coat he had worn on the night of the earthquake were a couple of sheets torn out of an exercise book. He had carried them on his stroll on the chance that he might feel impelled to write a sonnet (Petrarchan Sonnets were the only poetical form he attempted, because they were so regular, and even so he did them very badly) On The Setting Sun, or To a Hermit Crab. He had not done so, partly because he had forgotten to take a pencil too ; but now, when he had smoothed the crumples out these sheets would come in handy for his letter to the Archdeacon.

In the morning he gathered some purple fruit whose juice he knew from experience to be indelible, squeezed them into a bowl, and with a reed pen wrote as follows :

'FANUA.

'MY DEAR ARCHDEACON,—I am sorry to trouble you, but I must ask that the launch may be sent to fetch me away from Fanua. My ministry here has been a failure. I have converted no one, moreover I think that they are best as they are.

'I am aware that I shall seem to you an unprofitable servant, and I am prepared for reproof. But I must tell you that in my present state of mind nothing that you can say, either of blame or consolation, is likely to make much difference.

'I should be very much obliged if you could send with the launch a pair of stout black boots (size eleven), some collars (sixteen and a half inch), and a bottle of Aspirin tablets.—Yours sincerely,

'TIMOTHY FORTUNE.

'*P.S.*—Also some bone collar-studs. There was an earthquake and I lost those which I had.'

When the letter was written he put it away. His mind was quite made up as to leaving Fanua, there was no danger that a week's delay or so in sending off the letter would weaken his resolution. Indeed if he had consulted his own feelings he would not have delayed for an hour. But he did not wish to leave Lueli until he was quite certain the boy was able to stand on his own feet.

One thing was beyond doubt : Lueli would not try to kill himself again. He had been frightened by the dark look of Death under the water. Though he said nothing about his drowning or his rescue it was obvious that he had set himself to get on good terms with the life he had then thought fit to abandon. Never before had he been so beautiful, nor moved so lithely, nor sprawled so luxuriously on the warm grass. Sleek, languid and glittering, he was like a snake that has achieved its new skin. He was grown more sociable too, and with a quite new form of sociability ; for instead of seeking the company of others he exerted himself to make others seek his. Although his drowning had done him no harm whatsoever and he had never been in better trim, he chose to preen himself as an interesting invalid. At all hours of the day the youth and beauty of the island would appear with offerings of fruit and invalid delicacies. Since the Fanuans are a people unequalled in kindness and idleness this was not such a great tribute to Lueli's fascinations. But what was really remarkable was the success with which he imposed himself upon them as a young hero. Even Fuma, who had stood out against his pretensions for several days, laughing at him and pulling his hair and making sarcastic remarks about people who couldn't swim, suddenly dropped her sisterly airs and attended on him as devoutly as the rest. As though this were the last plum that he had been proposing should drop into his mouth Lueli began to feel a little better now ; was able to go sailing or swimming —not even the waters that drowned him could quench his love for water—or to take a stroll in the woods. Presently he was addressing Fuma as ' Child.'

If he had not so utterly forsworn meddling, if the letter to the Archdeacon were not put away in his coat pocket, Mr. Fortune might have yielded himself to a glow of match-making. Perhaps Fuma was not quite the girl he would have chosen ; perhaps for that matter Lueli's choice of her was not quite to the exclusion of other girls ; but having been so heart-rent over the defeated estate of that spiritless and godless boy whom even his own younger brothers had been able to tease out of the village, it would have been sweet now to abet the happiness of this triumphant young man.

As things were, Lueli's recovery must be the waving of the flag which signalled his departure. So one morning he set off to find Ori and explained to him that he wished to send a message by canoe to Maikalua. Would Ori as usual see about it and oblige?

Early in the morning the canoe was launched : and singing and shouting the boatmen set out on their voyage.

As he watched them depart Mr. Fortune had a sudden vision of a pillar-box. It seemed to spring up before him, a substantial scarlet cylinder, out of the glittering un-tenanted beach. He remembered how long ago, one August afternoon, he had posted a note accepting with pleasure an invitation to play tennis, an invitation which came from some people called Tubbs who lived at Ealing ; and how, having done so, he stood with the sun beating down upon him, just outside the station, with people jostling past him and the newspaper man shouting :

' Star, Standard, Westminster ! Surrey all
out ! '—wishing with despair that he could
get his note back, for it seemed to him that
nothing could be more distasteful than to
play tennis at Ealing with those rollicking
Tubbses.

But now he had no wish to recall his letter,
though he was still sick with the wrench of
definitely despatching it. His only thought
was to leave Fanua as soon as possible ; and
until the moment of departure came he
could not imagine how he would pass away
the time. Gradually the pillar-box faded
out before him and he saw the ocean-waste,
the narrow diminishing boat, the empty
indifferent sky. His head was aching again
and he put his hand to his forehead. There
was that deluded watch, mincing compla-
cently on. It was much better at passing
away time than he. Half-past seven.
Another thirteen hours and he would be
getting himself supper, and Lueli might
come in or he might not. And after supper
he would be going to bed. But if he fell
asleep too soon he would wake early with
another shining unending morning before
him. No ! It would be better to sit up
late, to midnight if possible. For time

passes more tolerantly at night when the body is drowsy and the mind tired ; but in the morning hours there is no release from one's faculties, and every second is a needle-prick to consciousness.

The sand had dribbled out between his fingers, he found himself staring at the palm of his hand. It would be the better for washing ; and he turned back toward the bathing-pool. While he was still the headache was not so bad ; but every step jolted it and sent a heavy sick tingle up his spine to jar against his temples.

As the bathing-pool came in sight through the lattice of ferns and bushes he paused, for it came into his mind that Lueli might be there with his friends. And dropping on his hands and knees he crawled through the under-growth, holding his breath and cautiously poking out his head from the greenery to scout if the coast were clear. He need not have been so discreet. The pool was empty. There was no footprint on the sandy rim.

He undressed and bathed his body wearily in the cool water—it was always exquisitely cool under the shadow of the rock. It did not occur to him that by going a little further he could drown. He hauled himself up on a ledge and began to clean his toes with a wisp of seaweed.

The shade on his wet limbs, the sound of the sea, the breathing murmur of the woods in the soft steady wind was comforting to his headache. He began to feel slightly lachrymose and a good deal better, and with the tenderness of a convalescent he watched the fish darting in and out of the streaming weed. Of course he might have gone himself by the canoe instead of sending his request for the launch. But though he now realised that it would have been perfectly feasible to have done so, something within him assured him that it would not really have been possible. Things must take their course : and thus to wait still in Fanua for the launch to come and fetch him away was the natural course for his departure. He could see himself leaving the island in the launch, but not any other how.

That bull-faced fish had dodged in and out from the weed a dozen times at least. It was as persistent as a swallow. His body was dry now and his headache smoothed away. Only the heartache remained ; and he was getting used to that.

All this while, as he was crawling through

the bushes, and cleaning his toes, and
watching the fish, there had been but one
deep preoccupying thought at the back of
his mind—the thought of Lueli and a longing
for his presence. It was on the chance that
Lueli might come down to bathe that he was
waiting now. And he imagined the conversation that must take place between them.

' Lueli, I am going away from Fanua.'

' But you will come back again ? '

' No. I am going away for ever.'

It would be quite simple—as simple as
that. ' I am going away from Fanua.'
Above all he was determined that there
should be no explanations. It would never
do to tell Lueli that he was going away because of him. No smirch of complicity, no
blight of responsibility should fall upon
Lueli, happy Lueli, who had done him no
wrong, and whom so often he had sought to
injure from the best, worst, most fatal and
affectionate motives. How could he have
so teased his misery with that idiotic geometry—a misery, too, in which he was the
agent, for it was through him that Lueli had
lost his idol. That was bad enough, at any
rate it was damnably silly. Though what
else could he have done? Something

equally senseless, no doubt. But what was
it to his behaviour in the hut, when the
idol lay between them, and Lueli crouched
in his last refuge of silence while he sought
with menaces and blackmailing to rob him
of his faith, and bade him cast his god into
the fire? Ah! of the two gods who had
perished that night it was the wooden one
he would now fetch back again.

But this he could never say. He must not
give any reason for his departure lest he
should at length fall into giving the true one
and seeming to involve Lueli in his own
blunders. ' I am going away from Fanua.'
That must be all. Little to say : so little
that he must postpone saying it till the last
hour came, the hour when one says good-bye.
And for that reason he must shun Lueli's
presence, hide from him if need be and crawl
through bushes ; for if he once allowed himself to resume their old familiar intercourse
he would not be able to keep back the words :
' Lueli, I am going away. I am going away
for ever.'

He said it aloud, and as it were heard the
words for the first time. He put on his
clothes and began mechanically to walk
back toward the hut. Then he had a good

idea. Since he was leaving the island it would be a pity not to go up the mountain and have a look at the crater. Very likely he would never have another opportunity of inspecting an active volcano.

It would be a taxing expedition, and not without danger. He put up some food, cut himself a stout walking-stick and gathered a bunch of plantain leaves to stick in his boots—for it was decidedly an occasion for boots. Preparations always pleased him, for he had a housewifely mind, and by the time he set out he was feeling, if not less miserable, at any rate a point or two deflected from his misery.

The new crater was on the further side of the mountain. He decided that the best way of approach would be to walk up through the woods by tracks which he knew and thence to skirt round under the foot of the crags, keeping against the wind in order to avoid the smoke and fumes. As he mounted through the woods he could hear, at first the sea and the tree-tops, presently the murmuring tree-tops alone. Soothed by their company and their shade he climbed on peacefully enough for a couple of hours, keeping a sharp look-out for rents and fissures ; for however weary one may be of life one would not choose to discard it by starving, or suffocating in a deep crevice as hot as an oven.

At last he came out upon the tract of scrub and clinker which covered the upper slopes of the mountain. After the cool depth of the woodland it was like a pale hell, a prospect bleached and brittle such as even the greenest garden will offer if one sits up and looks at it suddenly after lying with the sun strong on one's eyelids. After a moment of dizziness the garden will revive again, but the longer Mr. Fortune looked at this land-scape the more spectral and repellent it seemed. And because the air quivered with heat the face of the mountain side seemed to be twitching with fear.

There were the crags, some two miles away yet, but looking as though he could throw a stone and splinter them. They were not rhododendron-coloured now, but a reddish and scabby mottle. They reminded him of a group of ruined gas-vats with the paint scaling off them, standing in the middle of a brickfield. It smelt of brickfields too ; and in the place of the former sounds of the sea and the tree-tops new sounds came to his ear,

ugly to match the landscape, and of a kind
of baleful insignificance like the landscape—
far-off crashes and rumblings, the hiss and
spurt of escaping steam : the noise of a
flustered kitchen.

Now was the moment to put the plantain
leaves in his boots. Those which he had
gathered were faded, he threw them away
and gathered fresh. Then, with a heart
beating harshly and remotely, he set forth
on the second stage of his climb.

It was hateful going—slippery bents,
bristling scrub, sharp-edged clinker which
hurt his feet. He tripped and fell constantly, and when he fell the clinker cut his
hands. Twice he remained crumpled on
the ground just as he had fallen, gasping for
breath and cowed by the frantic beating
of his heart, which did not seem to belong
to him, behaving like some wild animal
which, terrified and apprehensive, is dragged
struggling to the summit of the mountain
to be sacrificed there. And as he went on
the brickfield smell grew stronger, and the
kitchen noises grew louder, and the sun,
striking down on him from the motionless
sky, striking up at him from the ground,
reverberating upon him from the parched

landscape, enclosed him in its burning net.

He remembered the story of the woman Kapiolani, the Christian convert of Hawaii. Followed by a crowd of trembling islanders she had gone up the burning mountain to manifest her faith in the true God. When she was come to the crater of Kilauea she had scrambled down to the very edge of the burning lake, and there, half hidden in clouds of smoke, she called on Pele the Fire-goddess, and flouted her, calling her an impostor and challenging her, if goddess she were, to rise up out of her everlasting fiery den and overwhelm her accuser with its waves. Pele did not answer : she sulked in the heart of her fire, powerless before the name of Christ. And when she had waited long enough Kapiolani climbed up again out of the pit and showed herself once more to the crowd who had been cowering at the crater-side, trembling, and listening to the loud voice of her faith. And when they saw her, they believed.

Her faith, thought Mr. Fortune, had carried her lightly up the mountain side, and over the lava-flow which she had trodden with scorched and bleeding feet. But he,

though a man, and born free from the burden
of heathen fears, and wearing boots, was
already tired out and reluctant, and only
a cold tourist's curiosity could carry him
onward, and a bargain-hunting spirit which
told him that having gone so far it would be
a waste not to go on to the end.

Kapiolani had made her act of faith in the
year 1825. And after that, as though for her
courage she were like the prophetess Deborah,
the land had peace thirty years. Then Pele
shook herself contemptuously, and fell to her
tricks again. At her first shake the island
trembled, as though it knew what was to
come. ' Yet a little,' said the Fire-goddess ;
and slept for another ten years. This time
she woke angrier. The island quivered like
the lid of a boiling pot ; a river of fire, flowing terribly underground, rent open a
green and fertile plain, and five times a
tidal wave reared up and fell upon the
helpless land. And once more Pele fell
asleep, but fell asleep to dream ; snarling
to herself, and hotly, voluptuously, obscurely
triumphing in a dream of what her next
awakening would be.

Kapiolani would not know of that awakening at any rate. It was to be hoped that

she had been spared the others. Simple
faith like hers would be cruelly jolted by such
ambiguities in God's law. She might even
have lost it thereby, as did Voltaire, another
blunt, straightforward thinker, at a rather
similar exhibition ; for she could hardly be
expected to take the subtler view of those
long-standing and accustomed believers who
can gloss over an eruption as a very justifi-
able protest against the wickedness of their
neighbours. And as for saying that it is all
a mystery—well, there is not much satisfaction to be got out of that.

These thoughts carried him over the last
mile, and looking up he was surprised to find
himself under the crags. He began to skirt
round them. Now the noises and the smells
were so strong that as he rounded every jut
of the crags he expected to come on the new
crater. Just as he had climbed on to the
top of a large rock a gust of wind, veering
among the crags, brought with it a volley
of foul smoke, which rose up from beneath
him and smothered him round, just as
smoke comes suddenly belching out of the
vent of a tunnel. He stood for a moment
coughing and stifling : and then the wind
shifted again, and the smoke lifted away

from him, and looking out underneath it he saw that he was come to the end of his search.

The rock on which he stood was the last westernmost redoubt of the crags, and before him extended the other side of the island of Fanua. Far off and strangely high up he saw the sea-line. The ocean seemed to fall steeply and smoothly downhill to where it broke upon the reef in a motionless pattern of foam. Stretching away down the mountain side was a long, serpentining slab of lava—the thickly-burning torrent which had torn apart the flanks of the mountain on the night of the eruption, wallowing downward with an ever more heavy and glutted motion until now it was solidifying into rock; a brutal surface of formless hummocks and soppy and still oozing fissures. Everything around was deep in ashes, and here and there little gushes of steam showed where the heat still worked under the outer crust. It was like the surface of a saucepan of porridge which has been lifted off the fire but still pimples and undulates with its own heat.

Another jet of smoke belched up. Holding his breath Mr. Fortune crept over the rock on his hands and knees and looked down into the crater.

By night the spectacle might have had a sort of Medusa's head beauty, for ever wakeful and writhing and dangerous ; but in the light of day it was all sordid and despairing. Thick smoke hung low over the burning lava, and thin gaseous flames flickered on the surface, livid and cringing, like the ghosts of bad men still haunting around the corrupting body. Below this play of dun smoke and shadowy flame the lava moved unceasingly, impelled to the south, on and on and over and over as though its torment were bound upon an axle. Every now and then two currents would flow into each other with a heavy impact, a splash and a leap of fire. And then it was as though it clapped hands in its agony.

Slowly, because he was cramped with having watched it so long, Mr. Fortune raised himself to his feet and turned away. He had no thoughts, no feelings. What he had seen was something older than the earth; but vestigial, and to the horror of the sun what the lizard is to the dragon : degenerate. Shuddering and cold he went down past the shadow of the crags and over the scorched expanse of hell-ground towards the woods, hastening, still having in his ears the growlings and concussions of the pit and with that foul smell still in his nostrils.

When he came into the woods he stopped and looked up. The green boughs hid away the skies. He was glad. He did not want to look at anything eternal just now. He sat down on a fallen tree. Moss covered it, and creepers and tree-ferns were springing out of it ; but he parted the ferns and creeper and scratched away the moss and put down his nose to snuff up the scent of decay. Everywhere in the woods was the odour of mortality ; it was sweet to him, like a home-coming. He lay down and buried his face in the leaf-mould, pressing his eyelids to the warm mouldering softness, trying to forget the rock.

When he felt better he went on again ; and coming to a stream he bathed himself, and ate some fruit. He was not very sure of his whereabouts, so to follow the stream seemed the best plan. It was a pleasant guide. He heard it singing ahead as he followed its windings. All this part of the woodland was unknown to him. It seemed very venerable and solitary. The solemn girth and glossy great leaves of the bread-fruit trees pleased him all the better because he was thinking of them as beings transient and subject to laws of growth and decay. They were steadfast, he thought, because they knew of their appointed end. They soothed him, bearing faithful witness that his own should be no other—that he too should one day lie along the earth and be gathered into it.

It occurred to him for the first time that now he would not, as he had hoped, be buried in Fanua. And as though the thought had called up a vision he saw what appeared to be a graveyard before him. It was a sort of pound or enclosure, built of rough stones. Whatever the purpose of the place, it was clearly unfrequented, perhaps forsaken ; for the mossy walls were breached and tumbled and the grass grew clean and untrodden in the entry. Overhead the bread-fruit trees mingled their large boughs like a roof of wings. He turned and went in. He found himself surrounded by ranks of idols, idols of all sizes and all fashions, idols of wood and stone, all very old, subdued with weather, moss-grown, with the grass tangling round their bases.

He knew well what they must be : in this
island where every one had his one own god
these were the gods of the dead. At the
death of their worshippers the gods were
carried here and left to their repose till they
too in their time failed and sank into the
earth. He remembered who had died since
he came to the island and peered among the
idols for some more recent than the others
which might be those of his acquaintances.
Yes, that was Akau's god perhaps, and that
pot-bellied fellow with the humorous squint
might be the god of poor old Live for Ever.
Only Lueli's god would never come here.

Sad Lueli ! Just now in his flourish of
youth and affability he might forget his lost
god and do quite as well without him ; but
one day Lueli would be growing old, and
then—then he would feel his loss. For the
day must come when a man turns from the
companionship of flesh and blood, be it
flesh and blood failing like his own or the
flesh and blood he has begotten, and seeks
back into the traditions of his race for a
companionship more ghostly and congenial
—old habits, old beliefs, old stories—the
things his childhood accepted and his fore-
fathers lived by. In that day Lueli would

need his god. The lack of it would be a kind of disgrace, a mutilation.

' I cannot go from Fanua,' said Mr. Fortune, standing among the idols, ' until I have given Lueli back his god.'

The knife hung round his neck : it would be easy to take one of the idols, re-trim its features, scrape off the moss and make a new idol of it. But a feeling of decorum stayed his hand. However, he might study them, for he would need an example. He spent half an hour or so in the enclosure, kneeling before the idols, examining the details of their workmanship and trying to acquire the convention. Then, for it was still afternoon, he spent some time wandering round in search of a suitable piece of wood. It must be about two foot long, straight, without knots, not so fresh as to tear, not so old as to crumble, of an easy grain to carve, and for choice, of a pleasant colour. He sought out several pieces and experimented on them with his knife before he found one to his liking. It was of rather dark, sweet-smelling wood, of what tree he knew not, for he found it lying beside the stream. A freshet must have carried it there, perhaps from the hands of some other woodman ;

for there seemed to be cutting-marks about one end of it.

He sat down and began to rough out the image he had in his mind : a man with a bird perched on his wrist, his head a little inclined towards the bird as though it were telling him something ; and seated at his feet a plain smooth dog, also looking at the bird, but quite kindly. After so many failures, great and small : the trousers, the introduction to mathematics, all his very indifferent attempts at cookery, boiled bad eggs and clammy coco-nut buns, the conversion of the islanders and the domestication of the parrots, it might have been expected of Mr. Fortune that he would put forth on sculpture with diffidence. But his heart was in it ; he had never attempted anything of the kind before ; and anyhow, it is the vainglorious people who expect difficulties. Mr. Fortune in his modesty supposed that cookery, conversion, etc., were really quite easy matters, and that it was only he who made a botch of them. So when after an hour or so of whittling and measuring and whittling again, he found himself possessed of a considerable aptitude for wood-carving, and the man, the dog, and the bird emerging from the billet with every promise of looking very much as he intended them to, he was pleased, but without any amazement.

He worked while there was light ; then wrapping the idol carefully in soft grasses and leaves and tying it into a parcel with vines he set out to follow the stream by starlight.

Now into the solemn caverns of the wood came rolling solemnly the noise of the ocean. Wafts of sweet scent wandered to him from flowering shrubs whose flowers he could not discern, and large soft moths brushed across his face. He was footsore and perhaps sorrowful, and he knew that soon he must quit this island which was so beautiful and romantic under its crown of horror, and go, he knew not whither, but certainly never again to any place like this ; but nothing disturbed his enjoyment of the hour. His thoughts were slow and peaceful, and looking up through the trees he saw the heavens without disquiet, although they were eternal. The stream laughed and ran joyously forward to the waterfall. He looked about him and knew where he was. The stream which had borne him such pleasant company was the same whose torrent he had seen wavering and distorted on the night of the earthquake.

He hitched the god a little closer up under his arm and turned into a path he knew. As he neared the village he heard voices not far off. He stopped. Yes, that was Fuma's voice : and the laugh—only Lueli could laugh like that. Standing in the darkness he blessed them. The god weighed on his arm, and it occurred to him that this was the first time he had ever returned from a walk bringing with him a present for Lueli. Lueli never came back without some gift or other ; he was as prodigal as his native clime. Trails of flowers which festooned the doorway and wound themselves round Mr. Fortune's neck whenever he went in or out ; shells, which were casually thrown down on his mat and ran into his sleep when he turned over in the night ; perfectly uneatable shell-fish because they were so pretty ; feathers and fantastic ornaments which he wore with gratified embarrassment round his neck. He too had sometimes brought things back with him, but things practical or edible : never real presents, objects perishable, useless and inconvenient, friendship's tokens, emblems of love, that passion which man,

for all his sad conscience and ingenuity,
will never be able quite to tame into something useful.

Well, at last he was making some atonement where he had been so remiss. He was
a poor hand at presents : an Englishman,
with a public school training still lurking in
his heel, he would never be able with any
sort of grace or naturalness to offer garlands
of morning glories or small gay striped crabs.
But he was doing his best ; he was bringing
Lueli a god.

When Lueli came into the hut Mr. Fortune
had eaten his supper and was almost asleep.

'Where have you been all day?' inquired Lueli. 'I kept on looking for you,
and wondering where you had gone. I was
growing very anxious, I assure you.'

'I have been to the mountain.'

'To the mountain?'

'Yes, right to the top of it.'

'Oh! did you see the flames and the
smoke they talk about? What's it like?
Are there a great many flames? Does it
make a great noise? Did you feel frightened? I hope you were careful not to fall
in. Tell me all about it.'

'It is a very impressive sight.'

'Well?   Go on!'

'I will tell you the rest to-morrow.   Now it is time you went to bed.   You needn't trouble about Tibby.   I've fed her.'

He turned over and fell asleep.   All night he lay with the idol close against his side.

For three days he worked on it in secret, chipping and scooping and shaving, rubbing it smooth with fine sand, oiling it, treating it as tenderly as a cricket-bat.   As he worked, intent and unflurried, strange thoughts concerning it stole into his mind.   Sometimes he thought that the man was himself, listening to the parrot which told him how the doom of love is always to be destroying the thing it looks upon.   At other times the man seemed to be Christ, and the bird on his wrist the Holy Ghost.   In these suppositions there was no part for the dog, save as an adjunct to the design, steadying the base of the composition and helping it to stand upright.   But there was yet a third fancy; and then the man was Lueli, the bird neither parrot nor dove but the emblem of his personality, while the dog was he himself, looking up at Lueli's bird but on trust not to snatch at it or frighten it away.

On the afternoon of the third day the idol

was finished. So far it had been his, the creature of his brain, the work of his hands. In an approving look he took his farewell of it, and dismissing it from his care he put it to stand upright on the rock before the hut. Then, moving very quietly, for inside the hut Lueli was taking his afternoon nap and must not be disturbed till everything was ready, he went to the bush by the spring where the red flowers grew. Of these he wove a rather uncouth garland, after the style of the daisy-chains that children make, but a daisy-chain like slow drops of blood. He arranged this round the idol and walked into the hut.

'Lueli.'

Under the smooth brown eyelids the eyes flickered and awakened. Lueli blinked at him, shut his eyes once more and stretched protestingly. It was all most right : he would hear the words as he should hear them, he would hear them as in a dream.

'Lueli, on the rock outside there is something waiting for you. Go out and see what it is.'

He was conscious of Lueli rising and passing him by, and pausing for a moment on the threshold. He sat down with his face to the wall, for he dared not watch an encounter that must be so momentous. Even the eyes of his mind he turned away, and sat in a timeless world, listening. Then, at last, he heard and was released—for what he heard, a murmur, a wandering wreath of sound, was Lueli talking softly to his god.

He made a movement to arise, and then stayed himself. This time he would not intrude, would not interfere. Lueli should be left in peace. He too was at peace, wasn't he? His atonement had been accepted, his part was done. Now there was nothing left for him but to go away. He began to reckon the days. His letter had caught the boat, he knew ; for last night the canoe had returned and Moki told him that he had seen the Captain and put the letter into his hands. That was two days ago, and so by now Archdeacon Mason had hitched on his gold-rimmed eye-glasses and was scanning the letter at arm's length in that dignified way he had, a way of reading letters which was as much as to announce : ' Whilst reserving my judgment I remain perfectly infallible.' At any rate by to-morrow morning he would learn that Mr.

Fortune wished to be recalled from Fanua :
for though the boat touched at two or three
ports before reaching St. Fabien, she was
never more than half a day out of her time.
By this reckoning the launch might be expected, perhaps to-morrow evening, perhaps
on the day following. Then the canoe
would push out to the opening of the reef
and dodge forward between two waves. He
would stand up in the canoe, catch hold of a
rope, push against that footing, buoyant and
unsteady almost as the sea. He would be
on the launch, looking at the neat life-belt,
and smelling brass-polish again and warm
machine-oil. He would be off, he would
be gone.

Outside among the birds and the sliding
shadows of the palm-fronds Lueli was
still talking to his god—a happy noise.
Mr. Fortune listened for a minute or two
and then went on thinking. He would
have no luggage and that was a pity, for
he felt the need for doing something
business-like, packing would have been
a solace. Stay ! There would of course
be presents : the islanders would not
allow him to depart without gifts. They
would give him mats, carved bowls and

platters, a pig-sticker hung with elaborate
tassels, a pipe. A pleasant people, and
very beautiful, with their untrammelled
carriage and arabesqued nakedness. He
glanced down at his forearm where he
had allowed old Hina to prick out a
vignette of a fish with whiskers. While
she was jabbing and chattering he had
thought : ' A man who has lost his faith
in God may perfectly well allow himself
to be tattooed.' After Lueli, Hina was
the islander with whom he had gone nearest
to a feeling of intimacy. In extreme old
age, as in infancy, distinctions of nation-
ality scarcely exist ; and Hina had seemed
to him very little different to any legendary
old lady in an English chimney-corner.
She might almost have been his god-mother,
grown so aged as to be grown gay, and
without her wig.

To-morrow he must go round and bid
good-bye to everybody. They would be
very surprised, very exclamatory : he did
not think that they would be very much
upset. If they had seemed rather unreal
to him, how much more unreal must he
have seemed to them ! They had been
on easy terms with him—they would be

on easy terms with anybody ; they had
accepted his odd ways without demur.
While he still preached they had sometimes listened, and when he ceased preaching they asked no questions. When he
was happy they smiled back, and when he
was parched with anxiety they had not
appeared to notice much difference. And
at all times they continued to supply him
with food and to perform any services he
required of them.

They had grown accustomed to him
but they had not assimilated him ; and
his odd ways they had taken as something
quite natural since he himself was an
oddity. His departure would affect them
much as if a star had fallen out of their
sky : that is to say, it wouldn't really affect
them at all. There were once three stars
where now you see two : there was once
a white man with a magic box which
groaned when he trampled it who came
to Fanua. In the course of time the few
remaining people who had seen the lost
star would brag a little about its superior
size and lustre, saying that there were no
such stars in these days ; and similarly
in times to come a black and white being

ten foot high and able to speak in a voice
of thunder for seven days and seven nights
might haunt the groves of Fanua. The
ginger-nuts, they too might be commemor-
ated in the fact that he fed men with
red-hot pebbles. All he hoped was that
they would not use him to frighten children
with. But alas! he was fooling himself.
There would soon be plenty of white men
to frighten the children of Fanua, to bring
them galvanised iron and law-courts and
commerce and industry and bicycles and
patent medicines and American alarm clocks,
besides the blessing of religion. The island
could not hope to keep its innocence much
longer. Had he not come, a single spy?
And soon there would come battalions.
Poor islanders! He almost said: ' Poor
flock! ' Well, to-morrow he must bid
them good-bye, and to-morrow too, before
he bade farewell to the rest, he must say:
' I am going away, Lueli, I am going
away for ever.'

And then—*suppose the launch didn't come?*
Suppose that the earthquake at Fanua
had been but a ripple of an enormous
earthquake which had swallowed up St.
Fabien?

It would not do to fancy such things. He got up and walked out of the hut. Lueli was gone and had taken his god with him ; maybe he had carried him off to the little copse where he had cherished the old one. Absently Mr. Fortune sat down on the altar. His hand touched something cold and flabby. It was the garland of red flowers which he had woven in order to give the idol a more festive and Christmas-tree appearance — for a present is a present twice over if it be tied up prettily. He smiled, and hung it round his neck.

He was still sitting on the altar when Lueli came strolling back for supper. He came singing to himself, and as he walked he tossed a couple of small fish from hand to hand.

' Why didn't you come and bathe too ? Look ! I caught these in my fingers.'

' How beautiful they are ! '

They were silvery fish with black and vermilion markings and rose-coloured fins. Their strange blue eyes were yet bright, and they retained the suppleness and shine of life. One does not admire things enough : and worst of all, one allows whole days to slip by without once pausing to see an object, any object, exactly as it is.

' We will have them for supper,' he said. ' I am sorry that I forgot to come bathing. But I 'll tell you what. There will be a moon to-night, we might bathe after supper by moonlight. Unless you want to go down to the village.'

' No. It would be a lark to bathe.'

The night was so mild that after bathing they lounged on the rocks, dangling their legs in the water, which felt even more surprisingly tepid because its black and silver pattern looked so cold. The ledge where they sat was padded with the soft tough growth of sea-plants. Out on the reef some gulls were complaining.

The shadow hid his own face but Lueli sat in full moonlight. It was a good moment to speak.

' Lueli, I am going away from Fanua.'

There would be no need to add : ' I am going away for ever.' Somehow, from the tone of his voice or by some curious sympathy, Lueli had guessed. He started so violently that he lost his balance and slipped off the rock. He swam a few strokes out into the pool and then turned and came back again and caught hold of Mr. Fortune's knees to moor himself.

'But if you go you will leave me,' he said, lying along the water and looking up into his friend's face. 'Don't go!'

'I must, my dear. It is time.'

'Are you going back to your own country?'

'Yes. I expect so. Anyhow, I must go. A boat will come for me, the same boat which brought me when I came to the island. Perhaps to-morrow, perhaps the day after.'

'Not to-morrow!' Lueli cried out, his face suddenly convulsed with distress.

Mr. Fortune nodded.

'To-morrow or the next day.'

'But why do you only tell me now? Now there will be no time to do anything, I can't even make you a pipe. Stay longer! Stay even a little longer! I thought you would stay for ever.'

'I'm sorry if I have left it too late. I did it for the best. I didn't want to spoil our last days.'

'But when did you know that you would go away?'

'A long time ago. A bird——' He

stopped. It would not do to tell Lueli
what the bird had said to him. He would
not understand, he was incapable of understanding, because he was incapable of
feeling that sad, civilised and proprietary
love which is anxious and predatory and
spoil-sport. Even now, despite his distress
at hearing that his friend was about to
leave him, he wasn't attempting to interfere
or to do anything about it.

' Lueli, you know how sorry I am to be
leaving you. I will not speak of it much,
I don't think we need upset each other
by telling our feelings. We know them
already. But I have one consolation. I
am not leaving a weakling, some one that
I should have to feel uneasy about. When
I think of you, as I shall do constantly, it
will be with admiration and confidence.'

He looked down at the face raised toward his. Affection, grief, the most entire
attention were depicted thereon ; but for
all these Lueli's countenance still kept its
slightly satirical air. And this, because it
was the expression most essentially and
characteristically his, the aspect that nature
had given him, was dearest of all.

' When I came here you were still almost

a child. How the three years have changed
you ! You are as tall as I am now, and a
great deal stronger. You are almost as
strong as Kaulu whom you used to tell me
about—Kaulu the strong boy, who broke
the waves with his hands and forced open
the jaws of the King Shark who had swallowed his brother. And you are intelligent
too, and as you grow older you will become
more so. Perhaps you may become as
wise and prudent as Kana, who rescued
the sun and moon and stars and put them
back into the sky. And when he held
up the sun the cock crowed. Do you
remember telling me that ? And as for
charm—why, I think you the most popular
young man on the island and the best-
loved. It delights me to see it.'

' You flatter me,' answered Lueli in a
pleased voice.

Then he sighed. ' I wish you were not
going,' he said. ' I shall miss you. I shall
miss you terribly. Oh, why must you
leave me ? ' And he hung his head and
kicked his heels disconsolately.

The water splashed up, drops of spray
fell on Mr. Fortune. He shivered, but it
was not the falling spray which chilled

him. What could he say, how was he to comfort this child ?

' Do you remember how I used to tell you about my God ? '

' Yes, of course I remember.'

' I haven't spoken of Him lately, and perhaps you have noticed that.'

' Yes.'

' Well, the reason why I didn't speak of Him was—I have lost Him. I lost Him on the same night that you lost yours, the night of the earthquake. No ! '—Lueli had made a sudden movement of inquiry. ' He wasn't anything in the hut, He wasn't any of the things that were burnt. He wasn't the kind of God that could be burnt. But He was the kind of God that could perfectly well be lost ; and, as I say, I have lost Him.'

' But perhaps you will find Him, perhaps He will come back. I—my god——'

Lueli's voice sank into a warm cautious silence, the silence of a lover.

Mr. Fortune put out a hand and stroked the wet head.

' No. I am quite sure I shall never find Him. But I have no doubt He is somewhere around, and that is why I am

telling you of my loss. Because, you see,
when I go I shall leave Him behind ; my
God will remain here on the island where
I lost Him. And while He remains, a part
of me will remain too. I do not leave
you utterly.'

' Like a keepsake ? ' ventured Lueli after
thinking it over.

' Yes. Like a keepsake. But rather more
than a keepsake. Almost like leaving part
of myself.'

' Yes. I think I understand.'

' So now do you feel happier ? '

' Not now. But I shall later on.'

It had not been anywhere near as bad
as he had dreaded that it would be. It
had even been a rather comfortable conversation, and one that he would be able
to look back upon with kindness.

The next day, the last day, was spent in
packing and leave-taking. The news of
his approaching departure was received
with genuine regret, and from every one he
met with such kind concern that it would
have been impossible not to feel gratified
even if he had wished to be above that sort
of feeling. Ori, Teioa, and the other
important islanders got up a farewell feast

in his honour. Speeches were made, his health was drunk, and afterwards Mr. Fortune sat on the best mats, flushed with praise and wearing as many garlands as a May Queen or a coffin, while presentations were made to him. A necklace of carved sharks'-teeth, bracelets of scented nuts, mother-of-pearl earrings, several pipes, spears, paddles and carved walking-sticks, rolls of tapa and fine mats, coloured baskets, polished bowls, sweetmeats and cosmetics, several remembrance-knots of curiously plaited hair, and charms of all sorts—these were piled up on his lap and all around him. Only Lueli brought no gift. He sat beside him, examining and praising the gifts of the others and pointing out their beauties.

' I do hope he isn't feeling out of it because he has brought no present,' thought Mr. Fortune. ' My blessed child, he is too generous to have anything left to give. But I can't bear to think that he might be put out of countenance. I could almost wish——'

At that moment he became aware that Lueli was no longer by his side. The conversation suddenly died down, there was a conscious, premonitory pause and people were looking toward the door of the house. They wriggled to either side, opening a sort of lane. And then Lueli stepped over the threshold, carrying a resplendent head-dress of straw-coloured and scarlet feathers.

Walking solemnly, with a rapt and formal face, he advanced down the lane, bearing on high the softly-waving and coloured crown, till with a deep bow he laid the head-dress at Mr. Fortune's feet.

' But, Lueli ! ' exclaimed Mr. Fortune, too much overcome for words of thanks. ' This lovely thing, this marvellous thing ! Is it—can it be—— ? '

' Lueli is your especial friend,' said Ori. ' It is right that he should make you the best gift.'

There was a loud hum of approval. Mr. Fortune raised the head-dress, admired it all round, and put it on. The hum of approval swelled into acclamations and loud cheers.

Then it was Mr. Fortune's turn to produce gifts. He had spent most of the forenoon going over his possessions, such as they were, and in between spells of working on the idol he had contrived to make an assortment of pipe-stoppers, tooth-picks, bodkins, and such-like small items. With these and the mother-of-pearl counters and almost all his buttons he was enabled to produce a tolerable array ; and though he apologised a great deal over their inadequacy there was no need to apologise, for the recipients were overjoyed with objects so distinguished and far-fetched.

The knife, at once his most personal and valuable possession, was naturally for Lueli, and so was his pipe. Ori received the magnifying-glass and his two sons the whistle and the flint-and-steel lighter respectively. To Teioa he presented the magnet and to Mrs. Teioa the medicine spoon. Lueli's mother went into fits of rapture over the measuring-tape ; Tekea, a handsome, rather taciturn fellow, who had helped a great deal with the new hut, was much gratified by the nail-file ; the Párnell medal was hung round Fuma's neck and the pencil-case round Vaili's. The pencil-sharpener he gave to Lei-lei, village sorceress, doctoress and midwife, who declared that it would be an invaluable asset. At the last moment he remembered Hina, the old story-teller. He gave her the wash-leather bag.

After songs and dances the party broke up at a late hour ; and still wearing his crown Mr. Fortune walked home with Lueli by moonlight. The other gifts he had left behind, for Ori had undertaken to see that they were packed properly, ready for the morrow. A night bird was calling among the trees—a soft breathy note like an alto flute—and the roof of the hut shone in the moonlight.

' Will you go on living here, Lueli ? '

' Of course. Where else should I like to live so well ? '

' I am glad. I shall know how to picture you when I am thinking of you.'

' When I think of you I shall not know where you are.'

' Think of me here.'

As a result of the party they overslept themselves, and they were still breakfasting when Tekea came running up to say that the launch had been sighted. Mr. Fortune became a man of action. He knew instantly that no one from St. Fabien could be allowed to set foot on his island. He gave instructions to Tekea accordingly :

a canoe might go out to the reef to keep
them in play, but no one was to be taken
off the launch on any account.

'What shall I tell them,' asked Tekea,
' if they want to land ? '

' Tell them——' What could they be told?
Small-pox, tigers, taboos, hornets in swarm ;
he ran over a few pretexts but nothing
seemed quite suitable. 'Tell them,' he
said, ' tell them I say so. By the way,
you might take them out a few bananas.'

Tekea grinned. He was an understanding fellow. He ran back to the village
while Mr. Fortune and Lueli followed at
a more leisurely pace. There was nothing
to delay them : Mr. Fortune was already
dressed in his European clothes, and the
feather head-dress was carefully packed in
a large leafy frail. Just as they were
crossing the dell he stopped. 'Wait a
minute,' he said, ' we never washed up
the breakfast things.'

' I can do that afterwards.'

' No indeed ! That would be dismal.
We will do it now, and shake out the mats.
There is plenty of time, and if there isn't
it won't hurt them to wait. They 'll have
the bananas to amuse them.'

Together they put all straight and tidy, folded up Mr. Fortune's island clothes, threw away the garlands of overnight and the unused twigs and vines that had been plucked for the packing of the head-dress, and removed every trace of departure. Then they set forth for the village once more.

Every one was out to see Mr. Fortune off and wish him good luck. The launch was outside the reef and his luggage was being conveyed on board. There was a vast amount of it, and it seemed even more numerous because of the quantity of helping hands outstretched to deal with it. It was all so exactly like what he had foreseen that he felt as though he were in a dream— the beach, the lagoon, thronged with excited well-wishers, canoes getting their outriggers entangled and nearly upsetting, hands thrust out of the water to right them, every one laughing and exclaiming. Every one, that is, except Lueli : Mr. Fortune had not been able to include him in his foreseeing of the last act. He had been lively and natural at breakfast ; but now he was silent, he was pale, he was being brave. 'If I say something cheerful,' thought Mr. Fortune, 'I may upset him. What shall I say?' At the water's edge he turned to him. 'Forgive me if——' He got no further for Lueli's arms were flung about his neck. Mr. Fortune gently patted him on the back.

He got into the canoe and the dream began again. The canoe manœuvred at the opening of the reef, it dodged forward between the waves. He stood up, he felt the sea sidle and thrust under him as the earth had done on the night of the earthquake, the rope was thrown, he touched the side of the launch, he was on board.

In the launch was the secretary, grown bald and corpulent, who immediately began to tell Mr. Fortune about the Great War, saying that the Germans crucified Belgian children, were a disgrace to humanity, and should be treated after the same fashion themselves.

Mr. Fortune sat listening and saying at intervals : ' Indeed ! ' and : ' How terrible ! ' and : ' Of course I have heard nothing of all this.' His eyes were fixed upon the coral reef where Lueli stood, poised above the surf, and waving a green frond in farewell. As the launch gathered speed Lueli's figure grew smaller and smaller ; at last he was lost to sight, and soon the island of Fanua appeared to be sinking back into the sea whence it had arisen.

Now the secretary was abusing the French ; and from them he passed to the Turks, the Italians, and King Ferdinand of Bulgaria. Mr. Fortune could not yet gather who was fighting who, still less what they were all fighting about. However, there seemed no doubt but that it was a very comprehensive dog-fight.

' Shall I go back to Europe ? ' he thought. ' I couldn't fight, but perhaps I might pick up the wounded. No ! I am too old to be of any use ; and besides, I have no money to pay my passage.'

The launch scurried on with a motion that might have been described as rollicking if it had not also been so purposeful and business-like. The paint which used to be white picked out with dark blue was now buff picked out with chocolate. The mechanic was a new one. He had stared at Mr. Fortune when the latter came aboard, and now he came out of the engine-house with a rag in his hand and began polishing the brass-work, turning round at frequent intervals to have another look at him.

' Perhaps he expected me to carry a goatskin umbrella,' thought Mr. Fortune.

The secretary displayed no such interest. He asked no questions about Fanua, a negligible peaceful spot, not like Europe, not to be compared to St. Fabien, where there was a gunboat and a fermenting depot for the Red Cross Fund. And as for Mr. Fortune, he had known years ago all that there was to know about him, and that wasn't much.

His conversation shifted from the wife of an ex-prime minister who was certainly in the pay of the Germans to the proprietor of the Pension Hibiscus who had attempted to charge for teas served to the ladies of the Swab Committee and was probably a spy. Meanwhile the island of Fanua was sinking deeper into the Pacific Ocean.

At last he stopped talking. Mr. Fortune knew that he ought now to say something, but he felt incapable of comment. He did not seem to have an idea left. Everything that was real, everything that was significant, had gone down with the island of Fanua and was lost for ever.

No. After all there was one thing he might ask, one small interest which had been overlooked in the pillaging of his existence.

' By the by, can you tell me the exact time ? '

He was an hour and twenty minutes out. A bad guess on his part. But perhaps it was not quite such bad guessing as it now appeared to be ; for he had spent three and a half years in Fanua, and his watch might well have lost half an hour or so in that time. It was a good watch once ; but Time will wear out even watches, and it had seen its best days.

ENVOY

My poor Timothy, good-bye ! I do not know what will become of you.